INFERNAL CORPSE

D.J. GOODMAN

SEVERED PRESS
HOBART TASMANIA

INFERNAL CORPSE

ONE

Megan Howzer stood on the rocky shore of Lake Superior, staring at the choppy, early November waters and wondering if she finally had the courage to jump in and let the frigid waves carry her out to her death.

Not for the first time, Megan reflected on how most people would consider that cowardice, not courage. It was her experience, however, that anyone who said that didn't understand how depression seemed to work. She'd read somewhere that lots of people started to look outwardly happier right before they committed suicide, much to the chagrin of their grieving family members. It was because they'd finally made the decision to do it, that they knew this unidentifiable pain and numbness was going to end. She suspected that might be bullshit, though. She couldn't imagine being happy most of the time. Instead, the depression held her down, much like if she were weighted by one of the large rocks she currently stood on. When she was like that, she couldn't do anything. She could barely leave the house. She had trouble making herself eat. All of existence was a thick curtain she was tangled in. It blinded her and kept her from escaping. So killing herself? That seemed courageous to her. It felt like it might be the only way to rip through that curtain and prove it couldn't stay wrapped around her.

But it's not the only way, she thought. *Just open up the bottle in your hand and take what's inside.*

She'd driven here directly from the pharmacy, *here* being the grounds of one of the vacation rental cabins outside of Mucwunaguk, Michigan. Her summer job all throughout high school had been cleaning a number of these cabins between rentals, and she'd come to love this particular stretch of the Michigan coastline. In the winter, it had always been even more of a sanctuary, provided she was willing to brave the treacherous roads and try ignoring the subzero temperatures. The Upper Peninsula didn't exactly get many tourists at that time of the year, so she knew she could be alone with her thoughts here. It was here she'd first thought about killing herself. It was also here that she'd finally decided to get help. It had only seemed appropriate that, when she made what she was sure would be her last choice between living and dying, she do it in the same place.

It's okay, the voice in her head said. *You can live. Really.* She had wondered for a while if this meant she was schizophrenic, but the psychiatrist had told her that particular illness didn't necessarily work that way, despite what the media said. The voice always sounded to her suspiciously like Angie Zwiersky, the first person Megan had ever had a crush on and the first clue that Megan might be something other than straight. She wasn't sure why it was Angie's voice she always heard as the comforting voice of reason, although it probably had something to do with the fact that Angie had been nice to her during a time when no one else had.

According to the doctor, there was nothing wrong with hearing that voice as long as it didn't tell her to do anything bad. It was a coping mechanism, apparently, one she'd picked up and latched onto over the years, giving that voice its own face in her mind, its own personality and mannerisms. Apparently, in the face of all her mother's drunken antics over the years, Megan's mind had decided that the best way to stay sane was to go just a little insane. And it had worked for a time. Then she had dropped out of college after only a year and she was back here, no job, not many friends, no real prospects for the future.

It's not always going to be like that, the voice said. *And the pills in your hand are the first step.*

Of course, Megan didn't expect them to work right away. She wasn't even sure if they were the ones she needed. She'd never taken this kind of medication before. Megan's mother had always been saying to her, ever since childhood, that any and all pharmaceuticals were toxic. Never mind that the woman was more than willing to pollute her body with enough vodka to drown a fish, it was prescription medications that were bad. Even now, Megan still thought she could hear that woman whispering to her, saying that would be bad, that she would be a tool of the industrial drug complex or some other such nonsense.

Megan opened the child-proof cap and dumped the prescribed dosage of one capsule into her hand. This shouldn't be that hard of a decision. When choosing between living and dying, it didn't make sense that a fear of a couple of little pills would be the thing to keep her from making a decision. But most fears people had weren't rational. At least she knew where hers came from. A part of her wanted to take the pills just to spite her mother for filling up her mind with garbage and conspiracy theories, but she knew that wasn't a good enough reason to do it. Whatever she chose here, she had to do it for herself, not for anyone else.

She looked to either side up and down the shoreline. Nothing but rocks, trees, and empty open water as far as she could see. To her left farther down, she could see the gentle rise of the Porcupine Mountains (a title she had always thought was something of a misnomer, since she had seen the Rockies and in comparison these were more like hills with delusions of grandeur). Behind her, past the remains of a long-dormant shoreline campfire and copse of scrubby trees, a path led back to the rental cabin, completely deserted for nearly a month now. There were a few people still in a cabin farther down the shore, she knew, a group of friends taking advantage of the off-season rates before the weather made coming this far into the boonies an impossibility. All this meant she was alone. She hadn't told anyone where she was going and no one would likely think to look for her here. If she walked into the water, it would probably be hours before anyone missed her. So this was it. After all her hemming and hawing, this was really the moment where she had to choose.

Maybe fighting this really was the more courageous choice. She popped the pill in her mouth and swallowed it dry. It would take several weeks of regular doses before she would likely begin feeling anything other than side effects, yet this still felt like an important moment. This was the moment she decided to keep living.

Megan took a deep breath, the cold air feeling sharp in her lungs. Okay, so she wasn't going to kill herself. Now was the time to decide where she was going to go from here. Maybe not make plans for her future, since plans had a way of getting fouled up. Goals, then. Things she could strive for. Things she knew it was in her capability of doing. She'd doubted herself for so long that she wasn't entirely sure what those capabilities were, but she thought now was a good time to start learning.

First, however, she needed to eat and find something to wash down that nasty pill taste. For the first time in what felt like months, she smiled.

You know where you want to go, the voice in her head said. *You know who you want to see.*

She did indeed. The voice's original owner, Angie Zwiersky herself, was also part owner of the Gitchigumi Café downtown. She would probably be waitressing right about now. And according to local scuttlebutt, she was not only currently single but had recently come out as bi. Megan wasn't sure if she had the flirting chops to catch Angie's eye. What she was sure of was that, after all these years, it was finally time to at least try.

Something exploded farther down the shoreline.

Megan almost lost her precarious balance on the slick rocks. Her sneakers slipped but thankfully found purchase as she pinwheeled her arms crazily. It wasn't just that the sound startled her. The explosion, while not exactly nearby, had been close enough that she could feel a shockwave in the air. She hadn't been looking directly toward whatever had exploded, but out of the corner of her eye she'd seen a flash bright enough that she'd had to look away. Once she was sure she wasn't about to end up in Lake Superior after all and the explosion's echo had faded out across the lake, she turned in that direction, thinking for sure that she would see something on fire.

There was no fire, but there was a thin wisp of black smoke curling in the air and getting carried away by the cold wind. It was about a quarter mile west down the shore, closer to the Porcupines. The vacationers had probably heard it, but she doubted they would be close enough to inspect it before Megan herself got there. That left the question, of course, of whether or not she even wanted to investigate.

Angie's voice told her no, that wasn't a good idea at all, although it wasn't very loud. It probably knew saying such a thing wouldn't work. Megan's curiosity was too strong, coupled with a fact that this was probably the most exciting thing she would see in

Mukwunaguk all winter.

Megan carefully worked her way off the outlier rocks to a more solid section of the shore then ran as best as she could over the stony terrain to the source of the explosion. She couldn't for the life of her figure out what might have caused it. There shouldn't have been anything out here flammable, unless the vacationers had left something out that they shouldn't. At least, whatever it was, it wouldn't have hurt anybody. The edges of Lake Superior at the beginning of November could feel like an empty land at the very edge of the world. No boats or ships would be crazy enough to be out on the water. Even the roads, not even visible from here through all the trees, would be more or less deserted until they were closer to town.

Whatever the explosion had been, Megan could see from some distance away that it had left something of a crater. It was right at the edge of the shore, a depression in the earth just close enough to the lake that the waves deposited a small amount of water inside it. The closer she got, the better she could hear a hissing noise, almost but not quite like a snake. This gave her pause until she remembered that no snakes would be out in this just-above-freezing temperature. No, the steam rising up with the last of the smoke told her the sounds actual origin. Something in the crater was hot, hot enough to instantly evaporate any water that touched it.

She slowed down, taking this fact in. The distance and the angle were such that she still couldn't see whatever was in the crater, but her first thought was that it had to be a meteor. The rocks were certainly scattered around it as though there had been an impact. But would a meteor have caused a flash like that? How big would it have to have been for her to feel the shock wave from a quarter mile away?

Megan shoved the pill bottle in the pocket of her coat, all thoughts about whether to live or die gone now in the excitement of the moment. If it was a meteor, maybe she could take it and sell it. There had to be someone that would pay for it. Weren't there websites that made jewelry out of such things? If nothing else, she could sell it to the Mukwunaguk Historical Society, yet another trinket in their crowded little museum for the tourists to coo over in the summertime.

She thought she heard voices somewhere beyond the trees. That would be the vacationers finally responding to what they had heard. If Megan wanted to get to the meteor first then she would have to move quickly. She wasn't quite sure yet what she would do with it once she was there, given that it was likely still way too hot to touch, but at least she would have first claim on it.

Megan slowed, though, as she got close enough to see over the shallow lip of the crater. She'd never seen a meteor in person, but she'd always been under the impression that most of them were fairly small, maybe about as big as her fist. Whatever was still smoking and steaming in there, though, was bigger. Much bigger. And while the smoke and steam obscured her vision, she was almost certain that the soot-darkened thing inside was moving.

She stopped, knowing well enough that she didn't want to deal with any mysterious moving object in a crater. She almost turned around and ran off, knowing full well from years of consuming media what happened to anyone bold enough to investigate mysterious circumstances. Given a few more seconds, that was probably exactly what she would have done, too. But as the temperature in the crater lowered and the hissing was no longer so loud, she thought she could hear something else, a voice.

"Help..."

Holy shit, there was actually a person in that crater.

Any thoughts of self-preservation vanished as she pictured the horrible mutilation that the person might be suffering at this very moment. The voice had sounded female, although hoarse and scratchy like she had been breathing in too much smoke. Maybe it was one of the vacationers after all. Megan had been so lost in her own internal struggle that she wouldn't have noticed if someone had snuck on down to the shore for a little quiet-time of their own. But if a person was at the center of it, she highly doubted the explosion had been from a meteor.

Megan pulled her smartphone from her pocket, aware that she might need to call 911, yet she wasn't surprised when she saw that it had no signal. There was a cell tower over on the far side of Mukwunaguk, but here the reception was always spotty. The tourists even kind of liked it that way, the lack of phones making them feel more isolated even in the height of tourist season where every cabin was completely full.

"Help," she heard again. Even though she was closer now the voice sounded more feeble. Megan suddenly wasn't sure she wanted to see the state of the woman. Whatever gruesome mess was inside of the crater would probably stay with her forever once she saw it. Yet she couldn't just ignore a cry for help. Her mother hadn't taught her much worth learning, but she had at least taught Megan that.

She skidded to a halt at the edge of the crater. She could see now that it was deeper than it had appeared from farther away, also wider. The smoke and steam had subsided enough that she had a fairly clear view inside it, even if that view didn't make a lot of sense to Megan. There was some water pooling at the bottom now that the thing at the center was no longer quite hot enough to instantly boil it away. And that thing was…well, Megan couldn't be sure. It definitely had the general shape of a human but there was no way it could be the source of the voice she'd heard. That would require the person to be alive, and nothing could possibly survive what this person had been through. The person's skin, right along with any clothing they might have been wearing, was charred right through. Megan thought she could see the muscles underneath, but even that was burned black. There were still veins of orange and red cracking through the charred outer husk, giving the illusion that whatever had burned this person was still working its way through the inner flesh. The strange thing was that there was no smell, though. Megan would have expected the smells of blackened skin and singed hair to stink up the air, but Megan smelled nothing more than the fishy tang of the lake water misting through the air.

"Help." The thing's dehydrated lips moved. She really was still alive, somehow.

"Oh dear God," Megan said, again checking her smartphone and fiddling with it in the hope that it had magically added some bars in the last few seconds. It still gave her the X that indicated no signal. Deciding that probably wouldn't change anytime soon, she put the phone back in her pocket. The only way she was going to get help would be if she ran back to her car and drove until she got back in range of the cell tower. Leaving this woman behind somehow felt wrong though, especially since Megan didn't see any way she was going to survive more than a few more minutes.

"Just...just wait there," Megan said, realizing how stupid that sounded even as it left her mouth. This woman was in no condition to go anywhere. She didn't even look like she could move her limbs. She was curled into a semi-fetal position, and the black and dehydrated muscles made her look like pictures Megan had seen of those mummies that would sometimes be discovered in ice. Megan went to the very edge of the crater and assessed whether or not it would be a good idea to go in. The sides of the crater weren't so steep that she couldn't get out, and in terms of depth it would only go up to her belly button. It was filling up with water faster now, though. In less than a minute, the woman would probably drown rather than succumb to the burns. Maybe that would be the more humane thing to let happen, although Megan didn't think she could force herself just stand by and watch that. At the very least, she had to try to pull the woman out, maybe even get her to say something about what had happened before she died.

Her skin still looked hot, though, probably too hot to touch. Megan pulled out a pair of winter gloves from inside her coat and put them on. They were rather flimsy and wouldn't protect her hands for long. They likely would, however, work just long enough to pull the woman out. She didn't look like she weighed much.

That thought stuck in her mind as Megan carefully stepped down the steep sides into the crater. Maybe it was the burn damage, but there seemed to be something odd about this woman's proportions. She looked like she hadn't had an ounce of fat on her body, and she looked smaller than a grown woman should. Holy crap, was this a little girl? No, Megan realized as she got closer. Two large yet still shriveled protrusions from her chest marked this woman as a full adult, or at least a teen who had been well-endowed early. Her back was messed up though in a way Megan couldn't quite identify, almost as though the woman had been deformed even before whatever happened. These were all details that Megan knew she shouldn't be dwelling on just now, though. She could wonder what it all meant later, after she'd given the dying woman what little comfort she could and the police were involved.

"Help." This time the word was barely audible. Megan stooped down in the growing pool of water and leaned her ear in close to hear whatever the woman's last words might be.

"Please," Megan said. "Tell me what happened." She knew this would be a sight that would haunt her for the rest of her life and every moment she stayed here was a little more psychological trauma added to her already heaping pile. Yet she couldn't leave yet. It was the only right thing to do.

The woman's lips moved again, but this time no sound came out. Megan moved closer, hoping she might decipher some of what she was saying through lip reading, but there weren't enough lips left to read. There was, however, something else odd about her mouth. Something strange about her teeth...

With lightning speed, the woman grabbed Megan by the shoulders with both arms. She sat up, her entire body creaking and cracking yet moving with a quickness that Megan had never even seen in a completely healthy person. Megan screamed, partly out of shock and partly at the red hot touch of the woman's hands that burned right through Megan's coat to singe the skin underneath.

"Help," the woman said again. There was no longer any sign of weakness in her voice. Her voice was strong, deep, throaty, and very clearly not human. Her charred lips curled back in a grim parody of a smile, giving Megan a clear view of the woman's teeth. All of them pointed. All of them sharp. All of them dripping with some kind of mucous-colored ichor like venom.

"Help me," she said again, then opened her mouth wide and came at Megan.

Megan's scream was short.

TWO

"No, I will not have sex with you," Angie Zwiersky said. Doug looked at her with a cocked head and a confused expression, as though he couldn't possibly consider a world where the words might be true. He was used to everyone giving him everything he wanted, after all. Simply hearing the word "no" shocked his system, especially when it came to Angie. He's spent a great deal of time wrapping her around his little finger, so to speak.

Doug licked his lips and let his tongue hang out. He probably didn't actually have the slightest idea what any of the words she's said meant other than "no," but he knew exactly the goofy expression needed to change her mind. He used this for exactly three seconds before he apparently forgot what he was doing and turned around on himself to lick his balls.

Doug was a wiener dog.

"No, I will not have sex with you," Angie said to him again. This time she didn't get any reaction at all from the dachshund, not that she expected or wanted one. She was just practicing, after all. Boris Romanov down at the credit union had been coming into the Gitchigumi Café for the last two weeks right around dinner time and demanding more attention from her than she was prepared to give at the busiest time of the day (even if "busy" at this time of year was a relative term). There was no mistaking what he actually wanted from her, considering his not-so-subtle hints. Of course, he hadn't cared about her one way of the other until she had come out as bi. Boris must have somehow conflated being attracted to both sexes with being easy. Angie's attempts to let him down gently had led nowhere. Now she was practicing a less gentle approach.

"Okay then, how about this?" Angie asked Doug. "Stop making passes at me or else I'll cut off your balls and serve them in the chili."

The mention of balls momentarily got Doug's attention, as though he were worried the balls about to come off were his own. Once it appeared that wasn't the case, he went back to joyfully cleaning them with his tongue.

Angie took a drag from her cigarette and then flicked the ashes away from Doug. The Gitchigumi Café had been smoke free since before Angie had ever taken her first puff, but they had never quite figured out what to do with all the smokers who still frequented it. Angie stood outside the back door on her break, using the dumpster next to her as her ashtray. Every time she did this, Doug appeared from wherever he went when no one was around. He always appeared well-fed and moderately well-groomed, yet no one knew who might own him or even if Doug was his real name. He responded to it, at least. Any attempt to catch him in the past had failed. He was just a cute, doofy little mystery that didn't mind Angie venting to him.

She stubbed out the butt of her cigarette on the brick wall, blew one last cloud of smoke into the frigid air, and then bent low to say good-bye to Doug. She'd try to pet him, but she knew from experience that he wouldn't let her touch him. Feed him scraps of bacon out of her hand, maybe, but that was it.

"I'll see you tomorrow, Doug. Don't worry. Your balls will be safe until then."

Doug chuffed as though to thank her, then waddled off between the diner and closed souvenir shop next door, vanishing to who-knew-where.

When Angie went back in, Rudy looked up from his newspaper just long enough to confirm it was her then went back to it. He was seated on an empty upside-down pickle bucket, a common habit with him that ensured he somehow always smelled like pickles even outside of work. Rudy was the head cook, a man of indeterminate yet definitely elderly age that had been part of the package when Angie had bought into the café. There were things he should probably be cleaning, but he never did any of that and pretty much ignored anyone asking him to. It was the kind of thing that might get him fired anywhere else, but here in Mukwunaguk his cooking was as much one of the tourist attractions as the historical museum or the lighthouse. Rudy might not be one of the owners of the café, but as far as most of the residents of Mukwunaguk were concerned, this place belonged to him just as much as anyone else.

Jasmine, Angie's aunt and partner in this particular operation, was in the back office working on paperwork. She ignored Angie completely, as she was completely immersed in the delicate operation of figuring out how to keep the café from going too far into the red now that tourist season was completely behind them. During the summer, the café hired on a few high schoolers to help wait tables or do the dishes, but at the moment the three of them were the entire crew of the Gitchigumi Café. They barely even had the money to pay themselves sometimes during the winter. Angie had learned the hard way in her first year as part owner to save as much as she could during the summer rather than spending all her extra money on frivolities, because by the end of the winter she might very well be living on canned beans and whatever leftovers the café wanted to throw away.

It almost wasn't worth being open in the winter at all, but enough locals still stopped in on a regular basis that neither Angie nor Jasmine would think of shuttering it. It was a Sunday evening, so that meant even the regular bunch would be diminished, but there would still be five or six that Angie could set her watch by, and probably a couple more that would stop by to take the sting off watching their football team lose about an hour ago.

Angie got to work making sure the ketchup bottles on each of the tables were full. Other than waitressing, that would be her exciting task for the day. Later, after the gray November day became a starless November night, they would close up the café and she would head home to curl up in with a trashy romance novel before passing out, only to wake early the next morning to do it all over again. It was a humdrum existence, everything she had been afraid of becoming when she was in high school.

Which made it odd that she had never in her life felt so alive.

The Gitchigumi Café had always been her fate. She'd known that ever since she was a tiny child. She'd been raised in this restaurant, more or less literally. After her mother had abandoned them, her father had tried to make ends meet however he could. Angie had a few vague memories of living in places other than Mukwunaguk before that, but her father had brought her back here to his hometown because, other than Angie, Jasmine was the only family he had left. She'd been running the café for a couple years by then, and at first her father had done little more than help out with odd jobs while he looked for what he called "a real job." He thought he'd be able to get work at the toothpick factory, the only real industry besides tourism that still existed here, but that had shut down shortly after they moved here. It was funny, thinking how that little bit of timing had affected Angie's entire life. Had he moved here just six months later, he probably could have gotten work when the factory was redone on a smaller scale manufacturing chopsticks that were exported to China.

Instead, he'd become more invested in the café. Her father had rarely been at home, especially after Aunt Jasmine had offered him half the business. Rather than spend her time as a latchkey kid at home, her father had made her come here every day after school. She would do her homework in one of the back booths, read, color, and generally entertain or annoy any customers that came in. Rudy himself said that she was another tourist attraction at that time, the whip-smart kid cracking jokes as a permanent fixture of the café. She'd even been featured in a travel magazine once that had come to do a piece on the museum and lighthouse.

As a teenager, though, she'd begun to chafe at small town life. It was typical, she supposed, to want to see what else was out there. It had bewildered her that people would come to this place on their vacations. Why would anyone want to spend their hard-earned money on Mukwunaguk? Was that decrepit old lighthouse really that special? Was there anything in the museum, if it could really be called that, that was worth seeing? Why would anyone want to visit a giant empty expanse of water? These people were fools in her mind and she, oh wise and great fifteen year old that she had been, was the only one who could see it.

Then her dad had died, and her life had been pulled out from underneath her. Aunt Jasmine was the one who took care of her for those three remaining years before she was legally considered an adult, and she had also been the one to give Angie her first job. Waitressing, of course. The tips hadn't been enough to save for college, though, and her father's life insurance had been pretty paltry. Her last couple years of high school had felt like a long never-ending funk that she would never get out of. There was no way she would ever leave this God-forsaken town.

On her eighteenth birthday, though, Aunt Jasmine had pulled her aside and revealed to her what had been a part of her father's will- his share of the business. He'd wanted her to have it, with Jasmine holding on to her share of the profits until she was eighteen. That alone wouldn't be enough for college, but Jasmine had told her that if she wanted to sell her half then she had a buyer in mind, an out-of-towner who thought he could turn the place into even more of a tourist trap. Jasmine hadn't exactly been thrilled about some of this guy's ideas, such as shutting down the café during the winter and adding to the menu, as Rudy called them, "frou-frou coffee drink shit." But Jasmine had been willing to make that sacrifice if it was what it took to make Angie happy. The savings plus the money from the sale would be enough that she could leave Mukwunaguk, maybe even go to college if she only went to a bargain-basement tech school. It had been all Angie's choice.

To the surprise of everyone, not the least of who was Angie herself, she stayed. There were occasions where she regretted the decision, but not often. She was more regretful that staying here had probably played a part in how long it took her to come to grips with her own sexuality. But she had grown to love the town itself, and the Gitchigumi Café in particular. She may have had a nearby apartment where she lived, but the café was her actual home.

There were plenty of times where she wondered what life would have been like if she had left, but she thought she had done well with herself. The money Aunt Jasmine had saved up for her went for correspondence courses, for everything from computer repair to learning Russian. She'd actually been more happy with that than she believed she ever would have been with a formal education. She knew a little about a lot, and she liked how that made her feel like she had a secret that most of the people around here would never get from her.

Although her dating life did suck. That much she had to admit. Beyond Boris and his feeble attempts to get in her pants, there wasn't much in the way of action around here.

And speak of the devil, there he was. Angie could see out the front window as Boris Romanov walked down Main Street, obviously heading straight for the diner. She supposed he was good-looking, in his own way. His nose was a bit crooked thanks to a fight he had once been in (he claimed it was a bar fight, but Angie had it on good authority that it was actually from a fist fight over a Power Ranger action figure that he'd gotten into when he was five), but he spent a lot of time cultivating a tall, dark, and brooding air about himself. Too bad his actual personality didn't match. He acted like someone who had seen the cover of one of Angie's romance novels, decided he could be like that, and then tried to mimic the covers without having even the slightest clue what was inside.

"I will not have sex with you," she muttered. For maximum effect, she would need to say it loud and with plenty of other people listening. Doing that to anyone else would have seemed mean, but after putting up with Boris's skeezy come-ons a little too often lately, she thought he deserved to be knocked down a peg.

Before he could even make it to the café though, the door opened and Kim Howzer walked in. She didn't walk in using a completely straight line, so Angie guessed she had to be on something illicit again, but the line wasn't quite wobbly enough to be booze. Angie would have guessed prescription pain killers if it wasn't for the woman's well-known pill-phobia. Angie wasn't a particular fan of the woman but she reserved all of her outright dislike for Boris and a few other rare people around town. Kim kept to herself and, except for the occasional paranoid rant, didn't bother anyone, although there was plenty of gossip that her daughter Megan had had a rough childhood under the woman's thumb. Angie had spent some time with Megan as a child, mostly out of sympathy, but Megan had pulled away from anyone and everybody at an early age. Angie still got sad thinking about it.

"Hi Kim," Angie said to her as she walked (although every move she ever made was more like a scuttle) to her usual place, a far booth right next to the one Angie had spent so much time in as a child. "The usual?"

Kim smiled and nodded, although she didn't make eye contact with Angie. She never made eye contact with anyone. Angie was pretty sure she would be hard pressed to find anyone in Mukwunaguk that knew the woman's eye color.

Angie went up to the order window that separated the dining room from the kitchen and yelled through it. "Kim's usual!" It was the normal ritual but ultimately pointless. Rudy had already folded his paper, gotten off his pickle bucket, and was throwing an order of hash browns into a pan.

As was usually the case at this time of day, Kim's arrival was like a seal had been broken, finally allowing other customers to enter the diner. Boris entered, sitting at a stool next to the counter so he could be within flirting distance of Angie whenever she needed to work the register. Angie yelled for his usual and Rudy threw on a couple hamburger patties and some bacon. Just a few minutes later, the Kincaids came in. On any other day of the week, they would have been all over each other as they sat in their booth, the perfect picture of slightly-inappropriate-for-a-public-place newlywed bliss. This was Sunday though, which meant Beth was wearing her Lions jersey and Kevin was in his Packers gear. Given the outcome of today's games, neither of them would be speaking to each other for the rest of the night, their entire dinner here going without conversation until, Angie assumed, their wild make-up sex made everything better between them later. They were some of the uncommon customers that didn't have a usual preference for their food and Angie had to perform the rare task of actually taking an order.

The Kincaids were followed closely by Old Bert (if he had a last name or had ever been known as Young Bert, it was apparently a secret he intended to keep to his grave). Angie got him a bowl of chili without even asking. A few minutes later, Becca Schuster and Johnny Hammerling came in, both of them inappropriately dressed for the weather in workout clothes. Becca was the yoga instructor at the town's one small excuse for a gym while Johnny was the place's most frequent customer. Becca was generally nice if a little on the spacey side. Johnny was super attractive, but Angie knew now that she would never see what he looked like under those sweats. An interesting side effect of her coming out of the closet was that everyone else suddenly seemed comfortable talking to her about their own sexualities or preferences. Johnny had told her that he was asexual and aromantic. His deep friendship with Becca was as close as he wanted to get to intimacy.

Angie brought them both salads and realized that would probably be it for tonight. Given the weather, which looked like it was preparing to give Mukwunaguk its first snowfall of the year, there might be one or two other people who would come in before closing to get a coffee or a hot chocolate or a bowl of soup, but beyond that these were her customers tonight. She set about to make them feel just as at home here as she did.

She managed to go nearly half an hour before Boris reached out over the counter and tried to touch her arm. Uck. Sometimes the guy had no sense of personal space.

"So how you doing tonight, Ang?" he asked. He'd never called her Ang before she'd revealed that she liked both men and women. Hell, he hadn't even called her Angie. She'd been Angela to him, very stiff and formal. Now, though, he seemed to think that his own pet name for her would be the straw that finally broke the camel's back. Or got her on her back. Something like that. Honestly, Angie wasn't sure what ever went through this guy's head, and she didn't think she wanted to, either.

"Keeping busy," she said out loud, but in her mind all she kept repeating was *I will not have sex with* you, over and over. She just needed to wait for the right moment. If she made the moment just embarrassing enough for him, maybe he would learn to keep his hands to himself.

"So busy that you can't get that drink you promised me after work?"

"Yep, exactly that busy," she said. In truth, neither of the two bars currently operating in town would still be open by the time she closed down the café tonight. The only place they would be able to get drinks would be at his place. Angie had no intention of ever learning what the inside of his apartment looked like.

She also hadn't ever promised him anything of the sort, but if she openly denied it she was afraid he would push the matter further, using some obscure, vague insult she'd given him at some point as proof that she had indeed promised exactly that.

"Come on, someone as beautiful as you has to have some other plans tonight. I want to join in."

"Beautiful, huh?" she asked with a raised eyebrow. Despite all his previous efforts, it was the first time he'd given her a real compliment.

"Well, fairly beautiful. You'd be much more stunning if you did something better with your hair."

Wait, Angie recognized that vague insult for what it was. Was he negging her? Using pick-up artist techniques? She's read about such atrocious things in some of her many random studies. The idea was to give the woman a compliment and an insult at the same time to get her to try fishing for more compliments. It was a move that was supposed to play with a woman's self-esteem.

It was a shit move, and Angie no longer felt bad at all for the embarrassment she was about to cause.

"You know what? You need to stop this," she said loud enough to ensure that every other person in the diner could hear her. "Why can't you take the hint? I will never have—"

She never got to finish the sentence, because she was interrupted by the crash of a car out on Main Street.

THREE

There wasn't a lot to the town of Mukwunaguk. Once, in the first decades of the twentieth century, it had looked like it would rise to become a major port on Lake Superior. The Great Depression had hit it hard, though, and the majority of shipping traffic on the lake had gone elsewhere. There was still a small harbor, although poor civil planning had played havoc on that: a breakwater had been constructed to keep the worst of Superior's winter waves from battering the boats docked in the harbor. This had led to the waves depositing large amounts of sediment in the wrong places, creating a peninsula that jutted out at a crazy angle into the water. The lighthouse, which had previously been essential to the town and ships, had consequently found itself nowhere near the actual water after a few decades. It had been abandoned for a while before being revived once Mukwunaguk became known as a nice place to get away during the summer.

The town itself was small, with only about two hundred residents calling it their permanent home year round. In the summer though, that number swelled to a couple thousand. Businesses that were shuttered during the winter opened. Shopkeepers returned, people with just enough money that they weren't sure what to do with it had summer homes, and a large number of people who spent the rest of the year farther south came up to Superior's shores to fill all the tourist's needs. Even the chopstick factory operated on a skeleton crew during the winter, mostly because they didn't have much other choice than to make do and didn't quite make enough money to relocate somewhere more hospitable.

All this meant that the streets of Mukwunaguk right now were eerily quiet. Most folks were holed up in their homes, wrapped in blankets with their heaters turned up to full blast for the first time this year. Maybe farther south some people had already had their heat on for all of October, but up here in the Upper Peninsula and especially on the shores of the Great Lakes, they were used to a little cold. Weather reports earlier had said that it was likely to snow tonight, although the weather woman had said it probably wouldn't be much more than a flurry. Anyone who lived on the Great Lakes, though, knew that the waters often had an unpredictable effect on the weather. No one would be surprised it tonight was the first real snow storm of the season.

Even with all that, Angie was still surprised that a few other people went out onto Main Street to see the accident. Granted, the crash hadn't been too loud, and judging from the state of the car there probably wouldn't be any serious injuries. Still, any unexpected noise at all should have brought out more lookie-loos. All she saw was Carol from the grocery store a couple doors down, who came out just long enough to see the car before pulling out a phone and calling the police. Angie supposed that meant she wouldn't have to be the one to make the call herself.

Angie was the first one out the door of the café, immediately going across the street to the scene of the accident while a number of the customers gathered just outside the door and watched. The car had gone up onto the curb and hit a light post, but judging from the amount of damage, it couldn't have been going too fast. From that, Angie would have expected the driver to be okay, yet the person in the driver's seat appeared to have passed out. It was difficult to tell in the fading daylight, especially since the light the car had hit was out while the others had recently switched on, but Angie thought it might be a woman. In a town the size of Mukwunaguk she fully expected to know the victim, although it still surprised her when she got close enough to open the door and Megan Howzer nearly spilled out. Despite her not wearing her seatbelt, Angie doubted the young woman's condition was the result of the crash. She was unconscious and pale, her forehead slick with sweat. Trying to touch her as little as possible just in case she was dead and this was some kind of crime scene, Angie reached out and pressed a couple fingers to the veins in her throat. There was still a pulse. Angie would have expected it to be weak, except her heart was instead racing so fast Angie wouldn't have been able to keep track of the beats.

She turned around and looked at the customers gathered in the door. Kim Howzer stood there behind most of the others, craning her neck in an effort to see if anyone had been hurt. As Megan's mother she had a right to see this, but given Kim's reputation when it came to her daughter, Angie thought it might be better for the young woman if her mother was kept at a distance for the moment.

"Hey, I think Carol just called 911 but could someone else do it just to be sure?" Angie called.

"Who is it?" Boris called back. He took a few steps away from the crowd as though to help. Angie would have rather not been anywhere near him, but she probably wouldn't be able to do anything for Megan all by herself.

"Just…shit. Boris, get over here. Aunt Jasmine, get everyone else back inside."

Jasmine had appeared at the back of the crowd and proceeded to herd everyone back inside. There were protests from most of them, but Angie knew people just standing around would be more likely to get in the way, even if they did stay across the street. Boris jogged on over and, upon seeing who it was, turned to look back at the café.

"Should we tell her?" he asked in a voice that only Angie could here.

"Not yet. Did anyone call?"

"Rudy did, I think."

"Come on, help me get her out of the car."

"Are you sure we should do that? I thought you weren't supposed to move an accident victim just in case they had a back problem or something."

Angie stopped and took a closer look at Megan. There wasn't anything that suggested Megan's state had come from the accident. It looked like something had been very wrong with her beforehand. In fact, there seemed to be some kind of wound in the cleft between her right shoulder and her neck. Angie moved in to take a closer look but recoiled at the stench of burned flesh that permeated the car. Holding her breath, she tried again and found what might have been a bite and might have been a burn. Or it could have been both, or neither. Whatever it was, it certainly hadn't been caused by the crash.

"I think she has other things to worry about than her back," Angie said. "We can't just leave her out here. It's getting colder by the second. She'll freeze to death before the paramedics can get here." And truthfully, she wouldn't even have the benefit of true paramedics. At this time of year, the best Mukwunaguk had was a volunteer fire department. They would give her basic first aid and then try to get her to the nearest hospital, which was about a half hour away if the person driving there ignored the speed limit.

Boris saw what she was looking at and tried to get a better look himself. "Holy shit. What even is that?"

"We'll ask that question later. Now are you going to help me or what?"

In order to pull Megan out of the car, they had to stand shoulder to shoulder, Angie taking ahold of her arms while Boris tried to dislodge her feet from where they were tangled in the peddles. Angie braced herself for Boris to make some kind of inappropriate move while they touched, but to his credit he kept his mind off of Angie's proximity and on the injured woman in front of him. Now that they were so close Angie took notice that Megan's coat looked like it was burned through in multiple places going all the way to the skin. The bits of skin that showed through the ragged clothing, though, didn't have nearly as much damage as her neck. In fact, those slightly red patches seemed incongruous with something that could sear right through fabric. As bad of shape as Megan was in, Angie couldn't help thinking that she should have been worse.

Once they had her free, they both gently laid her on the ground long enough for them to get a better grip on her legs and arms. While Boris took one last look inside the car for any other clues, Angie noticed that something had rolled out of Megan's coat pocket. Angie instantly recognized the small brownish-orange bottle for what it was and considered shoving it back into the pocket without even looking. Curiosity got the best of her, however. Angie picked it up just long enough to see what it was. A depression med, she knew right away. It looked like a pretty low dose, the kind that someone would be given when they were just starting. Angie knew this because she herself had a few very similar bottles in her own medicine cabinet. She'd been on this exact same med since around the time her father had died, although she herself took a larger dosage. Looking up to make sure Boris still hadn't seen it, Angie tucked the bottle back in the coat pocket as securely as she could, given the coat's state. This kind of thing was Megan's own story to tell, if she lived long enough to do so.

"Anything?" Angie asked as Boris pulled himself back out of the car.

"Her gloves on the on the passenger seat. They look like they've been burned, too. Christ Angie, was this an accident or did someone do this to her?"

He looked genuinely upset at the possibility of anyone harming someone else. It made Angie ease her judgment on him a little. Not anywhere near enough to sleep with him, though.

"Don't know," Angie said. What she could guess, however, was that whatever had happened, it was somewhere near the lake. The parts of Megan's clothes that weren't charred dry had a dampness to them, especially her shoes and the ankles of her jeans. She'd been standing in water recently. But considering how much of Mukwunaguk was on Lake Superior, that didn't narrow down her location much.

On three, they both picked her up and carried her across the street. They had to stop once and set her down when her legs began to slip from Boris's grip, but setting her down in the middle of the street was hardly the worst thing that could happen when there was zero traffic. They made it the rest of the way into the café without incident. While everyone had gone back inside, not a one of them had sat down, all of them straining for a choice spot at the windows to see the action. They saw what Angie intended to do and cleared away from a spot on the floor, giving them a place to set her down. Kevin Kincaid was the only one who didn't back away immediately, instead stripped off his precious Packers coat and balling it up to for a makeshift pillow for Megan.

"Megan?" Kim Howzer said. She was still standing near the back of the group, and Angie expected her to come barreling through at any moment. Instead, she stayed where she was, although she was visibly trembling. "Megan, honey, are you okay?"

Megan was very obviously not okay but no one had the heart to say it. Once Angie and Boris stepped away from her, she began to shiver violently, as though possessed by a frost permeating deep into her body. Yet Angie knew she couldn't be cold. She'd brushed the woman's skin as they had brought her in and it was uncomfortably hot to the touch. Megan was running a fever unlike anything Angie had ever seen. She didn't think it was even supposed to be possible for a person to be that hot and still live. Yet Megan was still clinging to life, proof that there was still a fierce will to live in that short, skinny body of hers.

"What should we do?" Becca asked. She fidgeted nervously, as though being so close to someone so obviously sick made her uncomfortable, but at least she didn't draw away.

"Who called 911?" Angie asked.

"I did," Rudy replied.

"And are they on their way?"

"Yeah, but they might not be here that quickly."

"What do you mean?"

"Tina said Bob and Louie were investigating another 911 call out by those tourists still near the lake," Rudy said. Tina was both the city hall secretary and 911 dispatcher. Neither was a job she usually had to do much in, but dispatcher was definitely her less common role. Bob and Louie were the police chief and his partner, two of only four actual law enforcement professionals the town bothered to keep on the payroll during the winter months. The other two typically worked the night shift, and likely would only now be waking up for the day.

Rudy's words immediately set off an alarm in Angie's head. During the summer, the town kept a much larger police force and a fully trained paramedic and fire team because there was actually a need for them. Tourists had a tendency to do stupid things in the name of summer fun, after all, and they often paid for it in the form of broken bones or drunk driving tickets. During the winter, however, it was considered eventful to have all of three reasons to call the police at all, with one of them inevitably being Kim Howzer calling in her latest conspiracy theory and demanding Bob do something about it.

For there to be two urgent 911 calls in a single day was simply not how it worked in the off-season months. Angie couldn't imagine any way that the two events weren't related.

As she looked around at the others, though, none of them

seemed as worried as she did. It would probably be best to keep her suspicions to herself for the moment, especially how half-cocked a couple of these customers would likely act at such a theory. Kim would declare it all an invasion by Big Government, while Old Bert would pull out his concealed-carry piece from its not-so-concealed place in his jacket and start waving it around in the name of "protection." Angie didn't hold with the idea that there was anything inherently wrong with guns and had met a lot of responsible gun owners over the years. Old Bert was not one of them. Whenever he drove Mukwunaguk's small tour bus from the museum to the lighthouse, he insisted on carrying the gun with him just in case one of the "city folk" tried to rob him.

"Did Tina say how long it might take for anyone to get here?" Angie asked.

"She didn't say much of anything," Rudy said. "She sounded rather flustered. She did say she would call in the volunteer fire fighters, but apparently several of them went out with Bob and Louie."

"Several" firefighters, in off-season speak, meant the majority of the volunteers. Help might arrive shortly, but it wouldn't be more than one or two people.

If that was all Angie was going to get, though, she would take it. All she needed to do now was make sure nothing happened to Megan in the meantime. The young woman still shivered, although not as violently as before. When Angie bent down and put a hand to her forehead, though, she had to pull it away. Whatever was wrong with her, it had beyond anything that could be called a mere fever.

"Maybe we should try sweating her fever out," Johnny Hammerling said. "Isn't that what you're supposed to do for a fever? Keep them covered until the fever breaks?"

None of the others had touched Megan yet so none of them understood exactly how bad this was, yet Angie didn't have any better ideas at the moment. She had multiple people strip off their coats and cover Megan up until she was in her own little cocoon, like a caterpillar preparing to turn into a butterfly. As a metaphor, it made Angie uneasy. Whatever was happening to Megan, she sure wasn't turning into a butterfly.

"Maybe we shouldn't wait for someone to come get her," Beth Kincaid said. "It might be faster for one of us to just drive her to the hospital."

"That might not be a bad idea," Angie said. "Who has a vehicle we could use?"

Becca raised her hand. "I could do it. I've got a Mustang. Probably won't find anything faster around here."

Old Bert snorted, muttering under his breath that his tour bus was faster than a Mustang could ever be, but no one else offered up anything better. Becca fished her keys out of her purse and ran out the door. Her car would probably be a couple blocks away at her home. Even with the cold weather, Mukwunaguk was small enough that driving down to the café wouldn't have been worth it.

"Help," someone muttered. The word was so quiet that Angie almost missed it. She stooped down next to Megan again and moved her ear closer to the woman's mouth so she could hear.

"Did you say something, Meg?" Angie asked.

"Oh. Angie. I thought you were gone. I was afraid you weren't coming back."

Well, Megan was obviously delirious but Angie took it as a good sign that she recognized her. "I'm here. We're trying to get you help. Just hang on."

"Help. That what's she wanted."

Angie blinked. "That's what who wanted?"

"The woman. Except I don't think…maybe it wasn't a woman. There was nothing between her legs. Not a pussy, not a dick, nothing."

Megan's mother gasped at hearing that kind of language from her daughter. Angie herself didn't hold much esteem for people who threw a fit over any kind of cussing. Language was a beautiful thing to her, even the words that were intentionally ugly. The exact nature of the words didn't make sense, though.

"Maybe she's trying to describe who did this to her," Boris said. Angie was about to say that they didn't know that a person had did this at all. She reconsidered when she took another look at the mark on Megan's shoulder. It really did seem to look vaguely like a bite, but not from any animal. It was, however, the perfect size for a person.

"She wanted help. I don't think…"

Megan trailed off, making Angie afraid that she was about to die, but it looked more like the effort of talking was tiring her out.

"You don't think what?" Angie asked.

"I don't think she was in trouble," Megan muttered. "I think she wanted help with…something…else."

Megan stopped talking and closed her eyes yet continued visibly breathing. Angie didn't think that would last for much longer though. Angie had seen death when her dad had died. It looked a lot like this.

For the next several minutes, there wasn't much else to do or say. A few of the customers went back to their tables and picked at their orders, but mostly they just stood around, glancing nervously at the girl on the floor as though this would be the time they looked and she was no longer breathing. She stayed unconscious but her breathing was surprisingly steady. Twice, Angie risked putting her hand back on Megan's forehead. The second time she thought maybe Megan had cooled down just a tad, but that could have been wishful thinking for all she knew.

"Shouldn't Becca have come back by now?" Beth asked Johnny. He shrugged as though he weren't worried, even though Angie could tell he was thinking the same thing. Becca's house was only a couple of blocks away, and she had been running when she left. Come to think of it, at least one of the volunteer fire fighters should have shown up by now as well.

"Hey Rudy, could you try calling Tina again?" Angie asked. "I'm starting to get worried."

"You're only starting now?" Rudy asked. "I've been worried for the last ten minutes." He did as she asked, though, going over to the phone next to the cash register and dialing. Angie went into the back to get her own smartphone from her purse just in case she needed it. There were dead spots all over Mukwunaguk, but here at least she had a signal if she needed it.

"Hmm. I wonder," Boris asked. Angie looked over to see him staring at her phone.

"Wonder what?" Angie asked. Instead of answering, he walked over to Megan and began going through the pockets of her coat. Angie almost objected, thinking he might find Megan's meds, but he found what he was looking for before he got to that pocket. With a smile, he took it out and showed it to everyone. Megan's own phone.

"So?" Kevin asked.

"So maybe she thought to get a picture of whatever happened to her."

"Smart," Angie said, although she loathed paying the guy a compliment. "Well? Anything?"

"Hold on a second," Boris said. He swiped a couple times on her phone. "No recent pictures, but it looks like maybe she took a video?" He held it up where everyone else could see it as he pressed play, but there was ultimately nothing to see. The image was nothing but a blurry gray shadow that occasionally jostled.

"She must have accidently started a video when she put it in her pocket," Beth said. "Probably not going to get anything out of that."

"No, let it keep going," Angie said. "She didn't get any video but maybe she got something on the audio."

Ignoring the image now, they all listened intently. Boris had to turn it up all the way for them to hear anything at all, and what they did hear was muffled.

"Sounds like Megan saying something," Johnny said.

"Yeah, but I can't make it out," Kevin said.

"Wait! Did you hear that?" Beth asked.

"What?" Boris asked.

Angie made a rewinding motion with her finger. "Go back so we can listen to that part again."

He did, and now that they were all waiting for it they could clearly hear another voice speaking. "Anyone recognize that voice?" Angie asked.

"Are you even sure it's a voice at all?" Jasmine asked. "Didn't sound very human to me."

Angie couldn't argue with that, but there was still a pattern to the muffled sounds that suggested speech. There were more noises that must have been Megan, sounds like rocks or stones clinking together, maybe even splashes of water. They all leaned in closer, expecting to hear something that would force this all to make sense.

Instead, they were rewarded with an ear-piercing scream, amplified by the fact that Boris had turned the phone all the way up. They all jumped back.

"Turn it off!" Beth said. "Please, turn it off."

Angie supposed there could still be more in the recording that they could use to piece this together, but even still she didn't want to keep listening to that scream as it continued. Boris turned it off and set the phone down on a nearby table, no longer so keen to hold it.

"Well, that was disturbing," Old Bert said. Angie noticed that during the recording he'd pulled out his pistol from its holster and had it sitting on a table nearby as though he expected to need it soon. Who knew? With the way things were going, Angie was starting to think he might.

FOUR

Angie had only been partly listening to Rudy's conversation on the phone, but the look on his face when he hung up told her it had not gone well.

"So?" she asked. "What's going on?"

"I could barely even make out what Tina was saying, she was so hysterical. But I got the gist of it."

Angie waited for him to say more, yet he seemed hesitant. He wouldn't even look her in the eyes, instead staring down at one of the salt shakers on the counter as though that would make whatever Tina had said go away.

"And?" Kevin said. He'd come to stand next to Angie beside the counter. The rest of the customers seemed to take that as a sign that they needed to congregate in the same place. The only one who stayed over by Megan was Kim, who stooped low but wouldn't get too close to her daughter. Kim was whispering something, either to herself or to Megan, but Angie couldn't make out what.

"She said she hasn't been able to contact Bob and Louie again. They reported in right before they got out of the car at the cabin but haven't said anything since. She tried ringing the landline in the cabin but no one answered, and none of the cell phones of anyone else who went there are working."

"Well, that's not ominous at all," Johnny said.

"Uh, I don't think that's the worst of it. That's just what Tina was able to get out before she started full on blubbering. It sounded like she was saying there's been other 911 calls all over town, or maybe it was just more on the west side, closer to that cabin out there."

Angie tried to control the sinking fear that threatened in her stomach. "And? What were they saying?"

"That's the part I wasn't really able to understand. Tina's words got kind of incoherent there, and then she just abruptly said she had to go. And she hung up."

"The 911 dispatcher actually hung up on you?" Jasmine asked.

"Yup."

Angie went over to the phone herself and dialed 911. The phone just rang. She tried City Hall's main number and got nothing there, either. After asking a few of the customers, she got Tina's cell number. That one went directly to voice mail.

"Johnny, what's Becca's cell number?" Angie asked. He told her and she called, but the results there were just as predictable.

"Holy shit, what's going on?" Beth asked.

"Back in the old days, I would say Commies," Old Bert said. "But these days? Probably ISIS. This is a terrorist attack, I tell you. They've finally come for us."

"It's Big Pharma," Kim said, not moving from her place at Megan's side.

"It's not Commies, it's not ISIS, and it sure as hell isn't Big Pharma," Angie said testily. "Wild speculation isn't going to help."

"Then what is it, little miss smarty-pants?" Bert asked.

"How the hell should I know?" Angie asked. "When did I get elected the leader here?" Nobody replied, although Angie thought she knew the answer. Whatever was going on here, she'd become the leader of this peculiar little group the instant she had taken charge of the situation after the crash. "First thing we need to do is stay inside," she said. "No one else is going out until we have a better idea of what's happening."

"What about Becca?" Johnny asked.

"I'm sure she's fine," Angie said. It was a lie, and from the looks on everyone's faces they all knew it. There was absolutely zero reason for Becca not to be back. They all seemed willing to accept the lie for now, though, as long as it meant that someone was stepping up and doing something, even if that something was telling them to do nothing.

"Maybe we should just send out a small group to look for her," Kevin said. "We could even keep cell phone contact the whole time."

"No," Angie said.

"Why not?" Kevin asked.

"Because splitting up is what stupid people do in the movies, and we already did it once. No, we wait. We can keep trying to call people, though."

Rudy sighed. "I guess I'll keep on that."

"How's Megan looking?" Angie asked.

Beth now stooped next to Kim. "She's not getting any better, but I guess she's not getting any worse."

"Okay," Angie said, a sense of panic beginning to set in as she realized everyone expected her to do something here, yet she had run out of ideas.

"Hey, I think I see someone," Boris said. He'd been staring out the window for the past few minutes in the direction Becca had gone. He pointed in the opposite direction, though, and Angie risked getting close enough to him again to look out. A few tiny white flakes had started to float through the air and would soon be thick enough to obscure her vision, especially since the daylight had all but faded to a hazy twilight. Through this, she thought she saw someone standing in the middle of the street, or maybe they weren't standing but walking at an incredibly slow pace. From this distance, Angie couldn't recognize who it might be, but she was immediately worried that anyone would be just walking down the middle of a street with an obvious storm approaching.

"Everyone stay inside," she said as she went into the back and got her coat.

"What, you're going out there?" Boris asked.

"Someone's got to find out what's going on some way."

"But you just got done telling us that splitting up was a bad idea."

"I'm just going to stay in front of the café. You'll be able to see me at all times. Besides, whoever it is they're more likely to need help like Megan than to want to hurt us."

"Hurt us? Someone wants to hurt us?" Kim said, much louder than was necessary. Angie sighed, reminding herself to watch her words a little closer next time.

"Just everyone stay put, all right? I won't be more than a minute or two."

Angie cautiously walked out the door. As soon as she was outside, she pulled out her pack of cigarettes and shook one out, lighting it before she went any further in the cold. Truthfully, this had been just as much an excuse to light up as it had been to explore this mystery. She wasn't even sure that she wanted to know what was going on. When she looked back at the café, though, she saw everyone's faces fogging up the glass as they watched, most of them probably expecting her to disappear just like Becca. Somehow the small town waitress had become the one all these people were looking to for answers.

"All right then, let's see what we can find out," Angie muttered, blowing smoke out the side of her mouth before walking toward the person in the street. She was mindful to keep herself within view of everyone inside. She also made sure to stay in the middle of the street herself. It wasn't like some truck was about to come along and mow her down given the way the weather was beginning to look, and she'd read enough suspense novels to know that, under strange circumstances, one should never get too close to out of the way nooks, crannies, alleys, or doorways.

"Hello?" she called to the person down the street. "Who is it?"

The only response the person gave was a couple of shambling steps in her direction before stopping again. Angie herself stopped in her tracks, not liking the looks of this at all. She was at least close enough now to see that the person was a man, although the increasing number and fury of snowflakes in the air kept her from discerning his identity yet. A quick comparison of the man's shape to every male she knew in town didn't help. Maybe he wasn't one of the townsfolk at all. She wasn't positive about who or how many tourists were still in the cabin out closer to the Porcupines, but it seemed possible that this could be one of them.

"You don't need to be afraid," Angie said. As soon as the words came out, she realized they were directed more at herself than at the man. "Do you know what's going on?"

The man started walking again, moving rather slowly but not stopping this time. Quite against her own will, Angie found herself taking a few steps back, despite the distance still between them.

The man was about six feet tall with glasses on his face and a ball cap on his head, but the closer he got, the more these details seemed off. His glasses were askew on his nose and the cap had dark spots on it that Angie imagined could very well be splattered blood. Incongruously, the man didn't have a coat on but rather wore a Hawaiian shirt. Despite this, the cold didn't seem to have any effect on him.

Angie backed away as quickly as she could without outright running. For all she knew, running would just invite the mystery man to do the same. Even as she tried to keep an eye on him, she nervously glanced around and behind her, very much aware that this had all the hallmarks of some kind of ambush. For a moment, she thought she might just be acting paranoid. Then she saw another one. Stumbling through the small parking lot next to the hair salon, she saw a woman. This one was close enough that Angie could tell for certain that it was a stranger. She was about Angie's size and maybe slightly older. Like the man, she wasn't wearing a coat, instead having only a pair of jeans and a t-shirt that said "Keep Calm and Ask a Librarian" as her protection against the elements. Like the man, her movements were halting and jerking. Unlike the man, she was very clearly injured, her arms covered in blackened bite marks suspiciously similar to the one on Megan's shoulder. Her skin was pale and her expression vacant. She didn't even look like she saw Angie, yet she still walked directly toward her.

Yes, Angie decided. This was very clearly the part where she needed to run.

No longer even bothering to keep an eye on the man, Angie turned and sprinted back to the front door of the café. A word was already starting to go through her head, a word that was completely ridiculous yet seemed to be the only one that fit what she was seeing.

Zombies.

Before she got to the door, Angie risked another look back. Another person (another zombie?) had appeared from somewhere behind the man. This was another woman with a purple stripe in her bangs and green cat-eye glasses, and if those glasses by themselves didn't give away her profession then her shirt, a perfect match to the one worn by the other woman, did. Angie had a stray thought – *Who knew Mukwunaguk was such a popular librarian vacation spot?* – before concentrating on opening the door and slamming it behind her.

"What? What is it? What's going on?" Boris asked. Angie

ignored him. She turned the lock on the front door and took a step back to examine it. The entire door was made of glass. It might have been a particularly strong type of glass, but it would still shatter if someone or something outside gave it the right motivation.

"Everyone needs to block the door," she said. "Something heavy that won't get pushed over easily." She realized she still had her cigarette in her mouth, then thought back to her smoke break earlier. "Rudy, run in back and make sure I locked the door."

"Young lady, I'm not doing anything until you explain what the hell's going on," Old Bert said.

What the hell was she supposed to say, that Mukwunaguk was being invaded by zombie tourists? No one would believe her. Maybe if they were all a little tipsy and it was the middle of summer they might think it possible, given how little regard one or two of them had for tourists anyway, but not now. Angie herself wasn't sure she believed it. This could still be some elaborate joke.

Angie looked over at Megan still prone on the floor. She didn't look so bad anymore, but there was nothing fake about her injury. This was not a prank. And there was definitely something wrong with those people out there, even if they weren't really zombies.

"I'm not even sure myself, but you've got to trust me," Angie said. She looked out the windows and saw the three tourists meet in the street then continue their slow shuffle toward the café. In the other direction, the one where Becca had gone, a third woman came into view, short with black curly hair and the only one wearing sensible clothing for the weather. Even as Angie thought that, though, the woman slowly shrugged off the coat as though she couldn't stand its warmth, even as the wind howled and the snow hit the windows hard enough to make numerous clicking sounds. This last woman had a few noticeable wounds, again similar to Megan's, although Angie could have sworn that they were steaming.

Kevin and Beth both gaped out the window at her. "Oh my God, what happened to her?" Beth asked. She must have realized the similarity between this lady's wounds and Megan's because she turned around looked down at the young woman with obvious dread. "Are we going to be safe in here with her?"

This was the first time that question had occurred to Angie, and she honestly couldn't give an answer. With the Z word still hanging around in her mind, she had a vision of Megan standing up when they all had their backs turned and making a buffet of their brains. But Megan did not seem to be in danger anymore. In fact, she almost looked like she could be recovering, just sleeping off a hangover rather than becoming a vector for a deadly reanimating virus.

Kim stood up and approached Beth, moving too far into Beth's bubble for comfort. "Don't you dare do anything to hurt my daughter."

Beth held up her hands in an "I surrender" gesture. "I'm not suggesting anything of the kind, Kim."

"We'll keep an eye on her but I hardly think she's the one we need to worry about just now," Angie said. "Now is somebody going to help me barricade the door or not?"

All of the tables were too small to be much deterrent and most of the booths were bolted down to the floor, but one mismatched booth in the corner that they'd added a couple years ago just to get more room for the tourists could be moved if they all worked together. The only people who abstained from helping were Kim, too wrapped up in the drama regarding her daughter, Old Bert, who said his back wouldn't be able to take it even though Rudy was around the same age and still helping, and Jasmine, who had remembered that she kept a small revolver in her office on the off chance that someone might try to rob the place and went to go load it. One bench from the booth was enough to block the door. The other bench could probably be placed across the other booths to block most of the windows, but Angie wasn't sure if they should do that yet. Maybe she was wrong about what was going on outside. Hell, logic dictated that she was almost definitely wrong. And if she was, then it would probably be important for them to see whatever might be going on. The windows were a weak spot in their defenses, but for the moment, Angie decided it was a weak spot they needed to keep.

The four tourists all met at a spot directly in front of the café. They huddled together like they were going to have a conversation, but their lips didn't move and they didn't even seem to be paying attention to each other. Now that they were all closer, it was quite obvious that all of them had wounds much like Megan's, albeit much worse and more numerous. It was becoming difficult to tell as the flurries grew into an outright storm, but Angie thought that she couldn't see any of them breathing.

Johnny was the first person to put together the same thing she had. "No way. Please tell me they aren't zombies."

"They aren't zombies," Angie said.

"Are you lying?"

"Maybe."

She waited for someone to say that wasn't possible, yet she wasn't entirely surprised when no one objected to the idea. In a small town like this, it was easy to believe in seemingly impossible things. Old Bert said he had seen a hollow apparition of a woman walk through a wall at the lighthouse late one night. Jasmine claimed she'd once seen some large, unidentifiable beast swimming in Lake Superior. Mukwunaguk was a town at the edge of the world, and at the edge of the world reason sometimes didn't seem so reasonable.

"So I'm assuming those have to be the tourists that were out at the cabin," Boris said. "Anyone know their names?"

Angie shook her head. "They haven't been in here. I think I saw them go into the supermarket yesterday, though. They might have told Carol." She thought about the woman in the grocery store right now, probably not thinking to barricade herself in like they had. If she got the chance, Angie might try to run and get her, but with the way these four were hanging around, she didn't think that would be anytime soon.

"Well, we have to give them names," Kevin muttered.

"Why would we need to do that?" Beth asked.

"Because we have to be able to identify them, don't we?" He pointed at the one man. "Archie." Then at the woman with the purple streaks. "Veronica." Finally, he pointed at the other woman in the librarian shirt. "And Betty."

"What about the fourth one?" Johnny asked.

"Weren't there three of them always fawning over Archie?" Kevin asked. "I could have sworn there were three."

"There were only two," Beth said.

"Are you sure?" Kevin asked.

"Jughead," Kim muttered from her seat on the floor. "The third one was Jughead."

"Um, I'm not sure that's how those stories went," Beth said.

"Is this really what we're arguing over right now?" Boris asked. "Old comic book characters?"

Angie waited for someone to propose better names, except no one did. It looked like those four poor people would be Archie, Betty, Veronica, and Jughead for the rest of their undead lives, if they all indeed were dead. Angie supposed that was the next task they needed to set for themselves: determining exactly how screwed up all this was.

"Some of them have blood on them," Rudy noted. "You think all of it's theirs?"

Angie hadn't thought about that, but now that she did, she realized it probably wasn't. While all of them were injured, the wounds looked like they had somehow been cauterized. There wouldn't have been much blood coming from them. Yet all of them had the signs that they had struggled with someone, and some of the blood looked fairly fresh.

"Do you think they did something to Bob and Louis and the others?" Jasmine asked, but before anyone could answer Johnny made a choked gasped and pointed in the direction Jughead had come from. A fifth person shambled down the sidewalk, but unlike the others they all recognized this one. She had, after all, been in here eating a salad only fifteen minutes earlier.

"Becca?" Johnny said. He went for the door and made to grab the bench, but Angie pulled him away before he could try moving it. "Angie, we've got to let her in. Those four might get her."

Angie looked around at the others, seeing from their expressions that most of them had already come to the same conclusion she had. "Uh, Johnny? I'm sorry, but I think they already did."

He stepped away from her, as though just being close to Angie was all it took to make the statement true. After a few seconds, his stunned expression became one of real horror. He went back to the window and looked out, finally allowing himself to see what everyone else had already noticed. Becca was in the middle of stripping off her coat. On her cheek was a blackened spot in the shape of a bite mark. She moved with the same slow aimlessness of the others yet still found her way into their little circle. None of them moved. They looked almost like they were waiting for orders from someone or something.

"This can't be real," Beth said. "This can't be happening."

Again, Angie looked around to see if anyone agreed, but almost all of them seemed to have accepted that something dark and supernatural was going on. They were still at a complete loss as to what.

Or at least most of them were. Old Bert had a crazy look in his eyes that Angie didn't like, the distinct appearance of someone psyching himself up to do something foolish.

"Bert, whatever you're thinking, don't," Angie said.

Old Bert sniffed. "And why not? You kids said they're zombies, right? Well, I've seen my share of zombie movies right along with everyone else. And we all know how to deal with a zombie."

He took his pistol out and cocked it.

"Oh shit. Bert, don't," Johnny said.

"You're not really going to let those kind of people invade our town, are you?" Old Bert asked. "This is our place. Just because they come here for a couple days or a week at a time doesn't mean they have any right to it."

"Bert, I think you are very much missing the point here," Angie said. She backed away from him as he swung the gun back and forth at them all. She didn't think he would actually shoot any of them. It was more of a gesture to keep them away from him. Yet Angie knew that if one of them didn't get a handle on this quickly, everything was about to go out of control.

"Do you have any idea how long I've had to put up with their kind in our town? In *my* town? They come in here and buy stupid little trinkets and act like they own the place, but I've been here since I was born. I'm sick to death of them turning this nice little place into a tourist trap."

"Okay, seriously Bert," Kevin said. "That doesn't have anything anywhere near to do with what going on, I think."

"It does!" Bert screamed. As if to emphasize his point, he aimed the pistol in the air and fired off a shot into the ceiling. Everyone screamed and ducked at the echoing boom and shower of plaster from the ceiling tiles. Angie made a note to make sure he paid for that, assuming of course they all survived long enough for him to.

"I'm going to put an end to this, and not a single one of you is going to stop me."

He aimed his pistol at the window and fired.

FIVE

Angie was afraid the glass would prove sturdier than she had thought and the bullet would simply ricochet about inside the café, but it shattered the glass and left a clear hole through the center of cracked spider webs. They could no longer see clearly through the cracked glass, though, so no one could be sure if Old Bert had actually managed to hit anything.

"Holy shit, Bert, put the gun down now!" Rudy yelled. Old Bert responded by twirling around and pointing the gun at Rudy's chest. Jasmine had her own revolver up in an instant and pointing at Old Bert.

"Point that somewhere else," Jasmine said. "I'm willing to bet I'm a better shot than you."

Bert looked around at them as though they were the ones acting nuts. "Are you people idiots? It's clear what's going on. This is the beginning of the end. The zombie apocalypse. And those outsiders out there are the ones who have brought it to Mukwunaguk."

"Are you including Becca as one of those outsiders?" Johnny asked.

"Yes! I'm sorry, kid, I know you and that girl have lived in town for a while, but you're still not from around here. You're not one of us."

"That has nothing to do with…" Angie paused. Was she really going to admit this out loud? Yes, she supposed she was. In all those movies and TV shows, when the zombies started to come, there was always a period of time where everyone denied what they were, as if they themselves had never seen zombies in the media before in their entire lives. Everyone always liked to say that they would be different if that time came. Well now was the time to prove it. "What you're talking about right now has nothing to do with zombies. You're just being a xenophobic shitbat."

Angie wasn't sure what confused him more, the fact that his waitress had just called him a shitbat or that he probably had no clue what "xenophobic" meant. Either way, he lowered his gun a little, which meant Jasmine also lowered her gun. So of course, that was the moment one of the zombies crashed through the broken window.

Angie had her back to the window and still had her coat on, so she was more protected as the glass exploded inward. She and the others shrieked, but she did it more out of shock than pain like some of the others. Glass showered Johnny's face, while Beth and Kevin put up their arms enough to block the worst of it. After the initial shock, Angie spun around to see Archie's fist jammed through the remains of the window, several shards falling and hitting his arm without causing any apparent pain. Through the hole he had made, she could see the other zombies behind him, with Becca the closest, all of them moving in a weird shamble that was somehow both frantic and slow at the same time.

"You idiot, you got their attention!" Boris screamed, presumably at Old Bert, although it was kind of hard to tell since he was running away from everyone toward the kitchen. That seemed like a good idea to Angie, who immediately began ushering everyone else away from the window. Old Bert and Jasmine both stayed put though, the two of them firing at the window with their guns. Archie took a couple bullets in the arm and chest yet didn't seem fazed. He did, at least, seem to realize that staying where he was would be a bad idea and pulled himself back out the window.

"Come on, everyone away from the window!" Angie said. Jasmine immediately followed her order. Angie expected Old Bert to argue and keep firing, but now that he had seen the zombie up close as it took a couple bullets without feeling anything, much of his bravado had apparently gone away. He stood there for a few more seconds, the pistol still aimed at the now vacant hole in the window, his jaw agape.

"It's true," he said. "They really are zombies."

"No shit," Angie said. "That's what we'd already said."

"I... I guess I didn't really believe it. I thought I was just shooting..."

Angie suspected his desire to shoot the thing that had come through the window was really nothing than a misplaced desire to shoot a few tourists, although she didn't want to sit and analyze that idea for long. "Get in back, Bert. We need to regroup."

It was fancy commander talk that she'd heard in movies. She didn't really know nor care what they were regrouping about or from or over or whatever. She just needed him to move someplace safer. Her commanding tone was enough to break him out of his stupor, though, and he shoved the pistol into one of his pockets as he followed her back into the kitchen.

Everyone had taken a position huddled close to the floor behind the order window. Angie shoved Old Bert down to join them and peered over the divider to see if there were still any zombies in view. The shattered window now had a hole in it large enough for someone to crawl through, although not without taking a serious amount of damage from jagged shards of glass. Snow fluttered in through the hole, becoming denser in the air with every second, and the wind blew through the hole and rattled the glass like an eerie, peculiar wind instrument. The darkness outside combined with the snow to make it very hard to see much of anything through the hole, but Angie thought she could see movement that wasn't just caused by the snow and wind. They were still out there, although she had no idea what they might be doing.

"Okay, so what are we going to do?" Boris asked Angie.

"How should I know? This is the first time I've ever had to face down a horde of zombies."

"I'm not sure there's enough of them to actually call it a horde yet," Kevin said.

"You don't think five zombies is a horde?" Beth asked.

"No."

"Well, then how many is a horde?"

"I don't know. More than five."

"You can't just make that claim. There has to be a specific definition of how many zombies it takes to make a horde. And I don't see why five wouldn't be enough."

"Because a horde is a horde. It's legion. It can't be just five."

"Then give me an exact number."

"I don't know. More than five."

Angie had seen them bicker like this before. There were two possibilities when it came to these two. One, they were about to start outright screaming at each other, which would last for less than a minute before they kissed and promised to make it up to each other later in bed. Two, they would just skip all that and go right to the inappropriate public displays of affection and it would be all she could do to keep them from tearing each other's clothes off and getting down to it right there on the prep table. Before it could get to either extreme, Angie shut them up.

"This is seriously not the time to argue about this," she said. She popped her head up over the divide again and instantly pulled it back down as she saw something in front of the hole, blocking the snow from getting it. "We have to figure out what to do."

"We should call 911 again," Johnny said. His voice sounded weak, prompting Angie to take a closer look at the damage he had taken from the exploding window. It didn't look like any glass had gotten in his eyes, so there was that much, but some of the lacerations looked pretty bad. He'd left a trail of blood droplets from the dining room to here, and they were beginning to make a noticeable pool on the floor. He was acting strong, but he needed medical attention. As far as she knew, none of them here had that knowledge.

"That's not going to do any good," Rudy said. "You didn't hear the way Tina was going on. I'd be surprised if she hasn't already run out of city hall."

"One of us has to know the cell number for Bob or Louie, though, right?" Boris asked. As he said that Angie looked up again, this time concentrating on the place on the floor where they had left Megan. They probably should have pulled her in back with them, but in their panic they had all forgotten her. She didn't look like she was in any immediate danger, though. The people who had been standing nearby had taken the worst of the glass, forming a fleshy shield around her. Some of the snow that had wafted in landed on her face, but it melted so fast that Angie couldn't be sure it hadn't just been rain. She actually seemed peaceful there, which was more than she could say for the rest of them.

Everyone shook their head at Boris but Jasmine, who seemed to be concentrating. "I think I still have Bob's number on my cell from that night we hooked up together."

"Wait, what?" Angie asked, then decided it wasn't really

pertinent. Her aunt could get it on with the sheriff all she wanted in her free time. "Never mind. Is your phone in your office?"

"I don't know if that's going to help much," Rudy said. "From what Tina was saying and the looks of those vacationers out there, I think maybe we're too late for them. They're probably wandering around somewhere looking for brains to munch."

Jasmine paled at that but said nothing, instead quietly going to the office to get her phone. In the meantime, Angie knew they had to come up with some kind of plan. It couldn't be that long before one of the zombies realized they could come right in through that hole.

"So how do we stop them?" Angie asked.

"All the stories and movies are usually pretty consistent," Old Bert said. "Shoot them in the head."

Boris gave him an obviously disgusted look. "And exactly how much experience do you have shooting moving targets in the head?"

Old Bert bristled. "Well I'll have you know that back in 'Nam I was—"

"Oh, don't even start that," Rudy said. "You already told me once when you were drunk that you didn't join the army until after the US was already out of Vietnam. You served as a cook in Germany."

"Well, I've still shot things in the head," Bert said, although he himself didn't sound sure if that was true.

"Okay, does anyone here have any real experience shooting moving targets?" Angie said. "Ones that are actually hostile, not just like deer or anything?"

Kevin raised his hand. "I've spent a lot of time playing *Call of Duty*."

Angie stared at him, trying to decide whether to shake her head at such a stupid thing or actually consider that as more combat experience than the rest of them. After a few seconds, though, she got the impression that something was missing from this scenario, someone not adding inane comments to the conversation.

"Hey, where'd Kim go?" she asked. Everyone looked around as though they expected to see her crouching right beside them, but she was nowhere they could see in the kitchen.

"She came in here with us," Beth said. "I saw her."

Angie cursed under her breath and looked over the divide again. Sure enough, she saw the woman creeping closer to Megan. She was keeping well hidden, though, using the tables and booths as cover from anything that might look in. In this case, the woman's paranoia was to her benefit. Angie saw a couple of ragged-fleshed fingers clawing at the glass, their state suggesting their owner had been worrying at the hole this whole time they'd been arguing. At least these zombies didn't seem to be the super intelligent kind, or else they already would have come pouring in. As it was, though, she didn't think the remains of the window would hold them back for much longer.

Jasmine came back in with her phone in her hand, but the look on her face already told everyone that no one had answered. Boris was right. Bob and Louis and every other person who had gone out to the cabin was likely dead right now and walking down the streets of Mukwunaguk. There were probably still plenty of people holed up in their homes or apartments, maybe even still oblivious to what was happening as the storm started to amp up outside. Most of them probably wouldn't be much help. Those of them who were stuck here had to come up with some other plan.

"Okay, so what do we know about zombies?" Angie asked. "Other than we need to shoot them in the heads."

"Well, they're slow," Johnny said groggily.

"No, not all zombies are slow," Kevin said. "The ones in *28 Days Later* were fast."

"Those weren't real zombies, though," Beth said. "Not like the ones in movies like *Night of the Living Dead*."

"Hey, news flash, kids," Rudy said. "None of those are real zombies. They're fictional. What we've got out there is not. We can't just make an assumption that they're going to be like things we've seen. We don't even know what's causing this." He paused. "Besides, everyone knows Romero zombies are the only one's that count anyways."

"Okay, before that note sends us back to ridiculous squabbling, let's just figure out what we do know for sure," Angie said. She thought about it for a second. "One, they can take a bullet without noticing it. So why are we assuming that a head shot will kill them anyway?"

"Because that's just always the way it works," Old Bert said, his tone clearly implying that this might the stupidest question he'd ever heard in his life, or at least the stupidest thing he hadn't heard from a tourist.

"Fine, fine. We'll let that assumption stand for now," she said. Looking over again, she saw Kim quietly dragging Megan away from the window. The fingers that had been groping at the hole were gone again, although she couldn't guess what that might mean. "Two, they can spread whatever they are to other people."

"Through bites," Boris added. Kevin shook his head.

"We can't prove that. We haven't actually seen them do that yet."

"But we've seen the marks, haven't we?" Boris asked. "They're all over the zombies, including Becca."

"Those don't look like any bites I've ever seen," Beth said.

"No, they're bites," Angie said. "I saw them closer than any of you, including the one on Megan. Definitely teeth marks."

"But why would they look burned, then?" Kevin asked.

"Don't know. But since those are the only really noticeable marks on any of them, let's go ahead and assume that's how it spreads. So far, it's a lot like the movies and stories."

"But that means that girl out there is going to turn, isn't she?" Old Bert said. "They always turn in the movies. There's no way to stop it."

Everyone else tensed at this thought. Angie herself wasn't so sure, but she didn't know quite how to voice her reservations. She didn't know how long it had been since Megan was bitten, but Becca hadn't been gone for more than ten minutes before she'd come wandering back as the apparently walking dead. Megan had been with them for longer than that, and not only had she not been getting worse, she'd looked for a while like she was getting better.

Old Bert looked around for, Angie assumed, Kim coming back. When he didn't see her, he dropped his voice low and said, "We need to shoot her."

"Nobody's shooting anybody else," Angie said. "I think we pretty well established that a couple minutes ago."

"Just think about it. They always turn. Every time. And there's always some schmuck that doesn't want to admit they're really dead and wants to keep them around, and then whammo! That person gets bitten and infected too. Keeping her around in this state is just a guaranteed way to get all of the rest of us killed."

"Bert, just shut it," Angie said. "No one is—"

"Maybe we should do it," Kevin said.

"Please don't start taking his side," Angie said.

"Look, we all know Bert is batshit crazy. Sorry, no offense," Kevin said.

"Plenty taken," Old Bert mumbled.

"But we do all agree that we're dealing with zombies here. And we all know the rules for how zombies work."

"But that's what I'm saying," Angie said. "We don't. We can't just go assuming—"

They never got to finish their argument, because that was when Becca came crashing through the remains of the window.

SIX

Angie wasn't looking when Becca came through, so she had no way of being certain, but from the way she was spread-eagled on the floor when Angie popped her head up to see, it looked like she hadn't jumped through so much as she'd been thrown through. This theory was supported when she looked out the now completely open front of the building and saw the four other zombies in two lines as though they had been using Becca like a battering ram. That by itself didn't match what most of them thought they knew about zombies. They weren't supposed to be smart enough to coordinate attacks, and yet somehow they had.

There was no time to contemplate that, though. The outside four were approaching the window while Becca was getting to her feet. Her face was now a bloody mess of lacerations, yet she gave no indication that she noticed. The people in the kitchen probably only had a few seconds before the zombies came for them.

"The back door, everyone," Angie said. "Hurry!" No one had to hear that twice. They all stood up and ran, although Old Bert hung back for a second as he first looked at the gun in his hand then out at the approaching zombies.

"Bert, no!" Angie said.

"I'm telling you, I can do this. I can end this all right here."

Archie and Jughead started climbing over the window pane with Betty and Veronica exhibiting a curious patience as they waited behind. The zombies lost all hints of intelligence once they were inside and on their feet. Becca, leading the way, shuffled along in typical zombie fashion. A little too typical, Angie decided. There was something noticeably familiar about that walk. Then Angie realized what it was.

That foot-dragging motion. It looked exactly like one of the dance steps to the video for *Thriller*.

What the hell?

Kim had managed to drag her daughter part of the way through the dining room without being seen, but there was no way she was going to get Megan to safety all by herself. One last time, Angie considered leaving her behind, seeing as she had already been bitten, but Angie's instincts told her there was something there she needed to know, some key difference that might help all of them in the long run.

"Fine then, Bert. Cover me," she said, then raced out the kitchen door to the dining room. Bert laughed and stood up in the serving window, taking aim at the nearest zombie.

"Let's see how you handle this, you undead bastards," Bert said. Even in her panic, Angie rolled her eyes. She reached Kim and grabbed Megan under her shoulders, directing Kim to take her feet. Kim was significantly less helpful in moving the girl than Boris had been, but Megan no longer seemed like nothing but dead weight. She moved slightly in Angie's hands, not fighting her but almost trying to help her. Any help she provided was minimal, though, and Angie knew this might take time they didn't really have. If she wanted to save herself, it was possible that there was no other way than to leave Megan behind.

Three gunshots went off in quick succession, and Angie looked up to see one hit Becca in the chest, one hit Archie in the crotch, and the third went wild. The zombies took no notice of their damage, although the shots did manage to get their attention more on Bert than on the three women struggling to get to the back door. The first three zombies shuffled right for Bert, completely oblivious to the fact that there was a counter and a partial wall in their way. Betty and Veronica finished climbing through the window and proceeded slowly toward Angie, Kim, and Megan. All the zombies had their arms out in that typical "walking dead coming to eat your brains" pose, although Betty and Veronica's arms were curled slightly, their fingers tensed into claws that swayed slightly to a beat that only they could apparently hear. Again, just like *Thriller*.

"I thought you were supposed to aim at their heads!" Angie yelled. She probably didn't actually need to yell, but her ears were ringing from the gunfire and that was the only way she could hear herself.

"I *was* aiming at their heads!" he yelled back. He seemed to realize he had some time now to aim, though, as he held the gun steady in front of him and took the time to make sure that this next bullet found its mark. With a softly muttered, "Sorry, Becca," he fired. The bullet went right into Becca's forehead.

All movement in the room seemed to stop for several seconds. Kim and Angie stopped to see what would happen. Old Bert stopped with a look of surprise on his face like he hadn't actually expected to get his target. The zombies all stopped and, in a decidedly un-zombie-like manner, looked at Becca as though they were expecting something.

Becca stumbled back, what little focus that had still been in her eyes going away as her eyes rolled back in her head. For a second, it looked like she was about to collapse. Bert even had a small smile on his face, as though this moment by itself justified every crazy thought he'd ever harbored about outsiders and he was just waiting for the moment when he could hoot and holler in triumph.

But instead stopping and falling, Becca burst into flames.

"Oh crap!" Bert screamed, his voice significantly higher than Angie thought possible. In a panic, he fired three more shots into the woman coming towards him, but despite the bullets and despite the fact that her entire body was engulfed in fire, Becca still kept coming. She moved faster now, jumping over the counter and reaching through the order window to grab Bert by the sleeve before he could pull away. Angie and Kim had managed to pull Megan most of the way to the back door by this point, which was open to allow everyone else to see the bizarre scene taking place inside. Angie directed Boris to take her place carrying Megan, then ran back into the kitchen in a last ditch effort to save Old Bert. Already things looked grim for him, though. After only a few seconds of being on fire, Becca was completely immolated, her clothes falling off in charred rags and making everything else they touched smolder. She seemed reduced, like the fire had made her physically smaller, and as Angie tried to pull Bert away from her, she held on, her rapidly dwindling body now light enough to get pulled right through the order window with him. The flames caught on his shirt and Bert continued screaming as the fire rushed over him with a speed that defied conventional wisdom. He dropped the gun on the floor as he fell back, Becca's charred body falling on top of him.

Angie instinctively ran for the fire extinguisher, but by the time she got it off the wall, it was obvious to her that there would be no saving him. Becca had quickly become little more than a blackened skeleton and some charred meat, yet she still held on to him as he batted at her. The flames rising up from them were so hot they burned blue, and everything else they touched caught fire right along with them. The small fire extinguisher wouldn't be enough to put them out anymore. Nothing short of a fire department could stop this now. And the fire fighters, Angie remembered, were most likely zombies by this point as well.

Her initial panicked thought was to simply drop everything and run out the back door, but she still had enough rational brain working to realize she needed to act smartly. She saw Bert's gun on the floor and went for it, making sure to stay away from the growing fire spreading throughout the entire kitchen. The blue flames from Becca had subsided in the more ordinary red and orange ones, but those had quickly spread to any flammable substance and surface around the two bodies. Bert still tried to scream, although the noise coming out of him was now more of a hoarse croak. Once Angie had the gun, she took enough stock of her surroundings to realize the four remaining zombies had made their way back to the front window. When everyone else made their escape, they needed to make sure they didn't go that direction or else they might all suffer the same fate as Bert.

With Bert's gun in one hand, Angie ran once more to the back door. Before she went out into the freezing storm, however, she took one last heartsick look back into the Gitchigumi Café. There would be nothing left of this place in just a few minutes. Everything she had done with her life, as insignificant as it might seem to others, was symbolized by this building. For a couple seconds, she looked at all her work going up in smoke and wondered if this made her a failure.

Then she remembered *Oh right, zombies*, and got the hell out of there.

SEVEN

Once they were all out and huddled next to a dumpster several doors down, Angie did a quick head count. Nine people here including herself. Most of them still looked pretty fit considering the situation, although there were a couple that made her worry. Megan was obviously the worst off, but Johnny also seemed to be fading thanks to a loss of blood. A few of them had their coats with them but most had left them inside the café. As native Mukwunagukers they all knew how to deal with the cold, but even people as hardy as them would need to get inside soon if they didn't want to freeze. Ironic, Angie realized, considering the blaze they were currently watching.

The Gitchigumi Café was currently a spectacular sight. It had only been one story and not attached to any of the other buildings around it like some of the older structures on Main Street, so it didn't immediately take anything else with it. The snow that was whipping itself into a fury around it probably helped to keep it from spreading. But even with these factors, the flames reached high into the early night sky. Angie wondered idly if that was just the way buildings burned or if it was because of the peculiar nature of how it had started.

"We need to get farther away," Angie said. "It still might spread to other buildings." And most of these buildings were old, after all, probably conforming to fire codes only by the most lax definitions. Without the growing storm all of downtown, Mukwunaguk probably would have joined it in less than half an hour.

"You'd think other people would notice one of the most famous places in town burning down right in front of them," Kevin muttered. No one else responded, although Angie had a guess why they weren't seeing too many gawkers. Partly it might be because they were still behind most of the main buildings and anyone watching would be in front on Main Street. But the zombies they had just encountered would not be the only ones roaming tonight. Others had probably been turned during that brief time where they had been holed up in the café. Maybe others had come across the zombies and thought to do exactly what Bert had. If this situation was typical, though, that would only result in more fires popping up throughout the town very shortly.

"We need to get somewhere out of the way," Angie said. "Anyone got any ideas?"

"We could go to my place," Boris said. Angie tried to pretend that she hadn't heard the not-so-subtle come-on in his voice, as though he honestly thought this was still a situation where he might get what he wanted from her.

"Maybe we shouldn't go to any of our homes," Rudy said. "For all we know, some of the zombies roaming out there might know where we live."

Kevin snorted. "They're zombies. They don't know anything. They're just the mindless dead."

"Yeah, well, zombies also aren't supposed to burst into flames when you shoot them in the head," Angie reminded him. "We can't make any assumptions about what they can and cannot do at this point."

Kevin murmured. "It kind of isn't fair, is it? The zombie apocalypse finally shows up and they don't have the decency to follow the traditional Romero rules."

Beth smacked him in the back of the head. "Is that really all you care about? Whether or not they're traditional enough? Remind me again why I married you?"

"Because I'm great in bed."

"Oh, right. There is that."

"I've got an idea," Jasmine said. "What about the museum?"

"Really? That's, like, a horrible place to hide," Boris said, although his voice didn't sound entirely convinced. Most likely he actually did think it was a good idea but didn't want to admit yet that he wouldn't be introducing Angie to his bedroom tonight.

"I don't like it in there," Kim said. "It's too…smelly."

No one could exactly argue with that point. The Mukwunaguk Historical Society Museum may have been one of the better known among the town's "charming" tourist attractions, but the word "museum" had never seemed like an appropriate term for it to Angie. It would be better to call it Mukwunaguk's musty attic, a place where the town's many curios and curiosities found their way to eventually and then sat in loosely organized piles, waiting for someone to come along and puzzle over them.

It was also, Angie realized, the ideal place for them to hide at the moment. It was large enough to comfortably fit all of them inside, and it probably wouldn't be the first place anyone would look for people at this time of night, or even this time of year, since it was pretty well shut up whenever there weren't enough tourists to justify keeping it open. It was also surrounded on all sides by streets and parking lots, meaning that if the fire from the café did spread to other places then the museum might be distant enough that stray embers wouldn't set it ablaze like everything else. Of course, if it did catch on fire, it could probably go up quicker than the café had. The place might as well have been a tinderbox, considering its collection of old newspapers, forgotten books on the history of the town, cardboard dioramas, and other easily flammable knick-knacks. Still, it was a better option than others.

"That sounds like a plan, but how would we even get in?" Angie asked. "The place is locked right now."

"Doesn't one of us have keys to it?" Johnny asked. "I could have sworn one of us worked there during the summer."

Kevin snorted. "Yeah. Bert. I'm betting his keys are in the middle of that," he said, pointing at the fire.

"I know how to get us in," Rudy said. "Sometimes when Bert would get drunk he would lose his keys, so he kept a second set around just in case. He told me once."

"Fine. Then that's where we're going, unless anyone else has a better idea?" Angie asked. No one answered. That settled it, then.

Before they could move, though, they needed to figure out what to do about Megan. There was still some grumbling from a few of them that keeping her with them might be dangerous, yet Angie said she was staying and everyone else at this point had, without actually discussing it, decided she was well and truly in charge. Occasionally, Megan would moan and move around, making Angie think that she might fully wake soon and be able to walk, or at least she might walk with some help, but for now they still needed to carry her. Despite Kim's insistence that she wanted to be the one who did it, Angie knew the woman wouldn't be strong enough to carry her daughter by herself. Hell, Kim was so willowy and malnourished-looking that she didn't look like she'd be able to carry much at all.

Angie also took a moment before they got going to check the states of both Bert's pistol and Jasmine's revolver. Jasmine's had three bullets, but Bert's was empty. In his panic, he had used the last of his bullets in a meaningless last second volley. Angie was loath to just toss the gun aside, though. In a town like Mukwunaguk where they loved themselves the Second Amendment, it wouldn't be too much of a stretch to think that they might come across more ammo. Angie wanted to keep the gun just in case and stashed it in the tip pocket of her waitress apron right along with her smokes.

Boris and Kevin took Megan while they quietly made their way behind Main Street's buildings, running between them quickly just in case Archie and the others were still out front in a position where they could see them. Angie couldn't even be certain that those four had escaped the inferno, but she thought it likely. For all their slow shambling, they had been quick enough when it counted.

That alone puzzled and disturbed Angie. There was something very weird about this whole situation. Or, at least, weirder than a sudden invasion of zombies on her small hometown should have been. What she had seen of the dead people so far – and she had no doubt by now that they were in fact dead – didn't quite seem to jive with what anyone would expect of zombies. Oh sure, in some ways they met expectations. They were usually slow and they couldn't be killed by conventional means. They even seemed to make more of themselves through bites. But in other ways, they were *too* normal for zombies, like they had been created by someone who'd watched way too much zombie media and didn't have enough creativity to add anything to it. After all, if zombies did spontaneously come into existence in the real world, what were the chances that they would actually follow any of the rules arbitrarily given to them in fiction? Did it actually make sense that a walking corpse could be killed again with a shot to the head? Who had decided these were the rules, anyway?

Of course, she had to remind herself that they didn't follow every rule, though. She'd never heard of a fire zombie before, after all. Still, all of this felt strangely formulaic so far. That might have been fine for fiction but the real world shouldn't be that easy to classify.

The museum was a couple of blocks down from the café and across the street. Angie decided it would be best to go those few blocks first, hopefully leaving the zombies close enough to the café that they wouldn't see the group crossing the street. The problem was she couldn't be certain where the zombies were now, or even how many currently roamed the streets. It could have just been the four tourists, or their numbers might have swelled enough that Kevin and Beth wouldn't need to argue anymore about exactly how many zombies it took to make a horde. Once they were behind the Sand Bar, Old Bert's former favorite place to get drunk and complain about the outsiders, they all stopped. The Sand Bar was directly across the street from the museum.

"One of us should go out front and see if anyone is out shambling around," Boris said.

Kevin put a finger on his nose. Beth immediately did the same. Angie, while recognizing the childishness of it, couldn't help but following suit. Johnny was next followed by Kim, who didn't seem to understand why she was doing it didn't want to be left out. Rudy and Jasmine were last, although they at least finally seemed to realize why they were doing it. That only left Megan, who obviously didn't count, and Boris, who looked thoroughly confused.

"Did I miss something?" Boris asked.

"You said one of us should go poke our head out front," Kevin said, making sure not to remove the finger.

"And? So?"

"So this means I'm not it."

"Me either," Beth said.

"Wait, are you people serious?" Boris asked.

Angie just shrugged. Not a one of them removed their fingers.

"Jesus Christ. What are you people, twelve?" He made no further complaint, however, just stooped low and moved slowly around the building to the front. Whether he thought it was stupid or not, even he had to respect the ancient mystical power of being Not It.

Once he was out of sight for the moment, they all put their hands down and waited. Angie still had her coat on so she didn't feel the wind digging into her bones quite as keenly as some of the others. Beth had also never gotten around to taking her coat off so she shared her warmth with Kevin, even if he looked distinctly displeased with huddling in a Detroit Lions coat. Rudy and Jasmine, neither of which had more than their diner uniforms, held each other tight in a hug that was somehow equal parts friendship and something more. Angie had never pried into their relationship, knowing they were closer maybe than they wanted to appear. Jasmine had least always had a very open idea of sex and relationships, making no apologies that she still had a very active love-life despite being on the older side. Rudy was probably even older still, but Angie wouldn't have been surprised to find out they had, at some point, been more than just boss and worker.

Johnny tried to get close to Megan and Kim for warmth, but Kim immediately pushed him away, citing the number of blood-borne diseases he might accidentally smear all over her in his current state. Angie took pity on him and gave him her own coat. Had Boris not been inspecting the front, she didn't think she would be as generous. Not because she didn't want to share, but because if Boris had seen her shivering, he probably would have used it as an excuse to make a move on her.

She tensed as she thought she heard something moving nearby. She wasn't the only one, either, since Jasmine had her gun in hand and ready in under a second. The others noticed and all went preternaturally quiet. After listening for a few more moments, though, she relaxed. She'd heard that noise plenty of times and recognized it for what it was. The click-clack of little nails on the pavement.

She bent low and whispered out into the snowy darkness. "Doug, is that you? Come here, boy."

A pause, then the clacking got louder and Doug trotted into view, his tongue lolling and his butt wiggling happily. The cold didn't seem to affect him, nor did he seem particularly troubled that her usual place to meet him several blocks away was burning to the ground.

"Good boy," she whispered to him. She put a hand out to pet him as usual, and just like always he backed away until he was just out of arm's reach. When she pulled her hand away, he came forward again, knowing full well that this was the point where she was supposed to give him a treat of whatever bacon or hamburger might have fallen on the floor.

"Sorry, Doug. I don't have anything for you." She sighed. "It doesn't look like I'm going to have anything for you ever again."

He plopped his butt down in the flurries accumulating on the ground and began to lick his balls, a clear sign of the disapproval he felt for that nonsense.

"It's really not safe for you out here," Johnny said. He probably wasn't as familiar with Doug's peculiarities as Angie was, because he tried to reach out and pet the dog himself. Doug appeared confused about whether he should run away or get closer, probably because he wasn't entirely sure if the blood all over Johnny's hands was supposed to be something good to eat.

"Yeah, probably not a good idea," Angie said, indicating the blood. Johnny sheepishly pulled his hand back. Doug stood back up and trotted off into the gloom. Angie figured that was the last she would see of him tonight, possibly forever if the rest of this night continued to be as catastrophic as it had begun, except after a few seconds Doug came back, sat just outside her reach, and whined.

"What is it?" Angie asked him.

"Yeah, is Timmy stuck in the well again?" Kevin asked.

"You know that never actually happened, right?" Beth asked him.

"What never actually happened?"

"On *Lassie*. Timmy never actually fell in a well."

"Bullshit he didn't. Everyone knows that happened, like, every week."

"No it didn't. As usual, you're wrong again."

"Not the time for foreplay, you two," Angie said. She reached out to Doug again. He still wouldn't let her pet him, but this time when he pulled away it looked like he wanted her to follow him.

"Yeah, no. I wouldn't do that," Johnny said.

Beth nodded. "Following a mysterious dog away from the rest of the group is a sure fire way to have your skull cracked open and your brains scooped out."

"Relax. I'm not going that far," Angie said.

Johnny's reply was choked and forced. "Yeah. That's what Becca thought, too."

Angie paused, fully aware that he was right. Doug looked like he was starting to get impatient, though, walking away a few feet and then coming back. He probably wouldn't stick around much longer for her to make a decision.

"Okay then. Someone else should go with me." She realized saying that was a mistake when several of them started raising their hands to their noses again. "Kevin. You're coming with."

"Me? Why me?"

"Because I said so." Jesus, it was just like leading a group of children. "Everyone stay put. I don't think this will take too long."

She actually wasn't sure of anything of the sort. Angie just said it more out of wishful thinking. With Kevin by her side, she followed Doug, still keeping low and in the shadows as much as possible. Thankfully, she had been right. Doug led them around a building not even a full block away and stopped. He set his little butt down in the snow again and looked for all the world like he was having a grand old time, yet a low growl emanated from the back of his throat. Angie walked a little ways past him, trying to see whatever the dog wanted to point out. The side street they were facing was completely empty.

"I don't get it," Angie said.

"Uh, I think maybe he has a problem with that," Kevin said, pointing at something on the sidewalk just ahead. Angie took a few steps closer but stopped at an inexplicable wall of steaming heat in front of her.

"What the hell?" she asked. Kevin joined her as she moved closer to investigate. Doug gave one short and yipping bark before running as fast as his tiny little legs could take him. Angie didn't bother to try following him. This was obviously what had spooked the dog so much. Now she just needed to figure out what *this* even was.

They were footprints. That much was obvious just from the

size, shape, and spacing. The footprints of what, though, she had no idea. Whatever it was, it certainly walked on two legs, so it was more likely to be a human than any animal. They weren't shoeprints, though, but actual bare feet. Five toes, a heel, an arch. They were strangely thin and elongated, though, especially at the ends of the toes where they looked like they might just end in points. The footprints formed a relatively straight line down the sidewalk heading toward Main Street and vanishing out of sight between two street lights.

None of that, however, was the most startling detail. What gave Angie pause and made her doubt her own senses was the fact that the footprints had actually been burned into the sidewalk. How hot would someone's feet even need to be to cause that? Probably hotter than anyone should have been while still able to survive. And judging from the dull red glow that some of them still had farther down, whoever had made them had only passed by a minute or so ago.

"Was…was that maybe… I don't know, Becca?" Kevin asked. The tone of his voice made it obvious that he knew it definitely hadn't been her.

"We need to get back to the others," Angie said. "Now. Then we'll go hide out in the museum and see it we can come up with some kind of plan."

"Yeah, you don't need to tell me twice," Kevin said.

EIGHT

Angie led the way back to find that Boris had returned. He looked impatient.

"What the hell you two? Main Street is clear but I don't know for how long. We don't have time for whatever..." Something on their faces must have given him pause. "What? What is it?"

"We'll tell you once we're safe inside the museum," she said. She gestured for him to lead the way. Megan was still groggy and incoherent, but she had apparently come to enough in the meantime that two people standing on either side of her could coax her into something that sleepily resembled walking. Angie paused at Main Street, looking both directions for any sign of the zombies, but everything was quiet. Eerily quiet. There were apartments on the second stories of some of these shop buildings, but she didn't see lights shining out of a single one of them. She didn't know what that might mean, nor did she care to speculate just now. They could discuss all these things together once they were inside.

With a name like the Mukwunaguk Historical Society Museum, an outsider might have expected something grander, or at the very least slightly flashy. In truth, it was an old converted Piggly Wiggly built in the seventies and, despite a number of paint-jobs and add-ons over the years, still had a blocky and outdated vibe to the design. Not that it was dilapidated by any means. A lot of local funds had gone into preserving both this place and the lighthouse at the edge of town. They were Mukwunaguk's main attractions, after all, when the tourists wanted something other than Lake Superior itself. Through the glass door facing the parking lot, Angie could see into the vestibule with a rack of brochures for various attractions around the Upper Peninsula right next to a series of quarter-operated dispensers that ejected plastic bubbles full of cheap trinkets for the kids. The inside was completely dark as it had been for the last couple weeks, the only people typically going in and out during this time being the exterminators, making sure mice didn't make nests of the various "exhibits" within. There was a locked garage near the back of the parking lot that got Angie to thinking, but before she could dwell on the beginnings of an idea, Boris spoke up.

"So Rudy? How are we supposed to get in?"

"Simple," he said. In a planter ridden with dead weeds next to the door, Rudy rifled through some of the stones around the bottom until he came up with one that was very clearly plastic.

"A fake rock?" Johnny asked. "You mean to tell me that the only thing keeping people from getting in and stealing everything from the town's history has been a piece of plastic this whole time?"

"Come on, kid. You know better," Rudy said as he slid the bottom of the fake rock open and pulled out a key. "There probably isn't a single thing in this entire building that anybody would actually want to steal for real."

Angie wasn't sure if she would go that far. There might be some things that out-of-towners might find interesting enough that they might try to walk away with them shoved under their coats, but when it came to Mukwunagukers he was mostly right. To the people who had seen it all a thousand times before, the precious artifacts of the museum were little more than trash, not even worth the effort of trying to hide them on the way out. It was even a time-honored and somewhat tolerated tradition among local teenagers to try taking things out and then sneaking them back in. The couple that usually ran the museum was aware of this, just as they knew damn well when some bottle or tattered book was hidden in some teen girl's purse. They knew who took each item by name and would give them a whole week to keep the item and brag about it. If it wasn't back after that, well, everyone knew that particular kid's parents, and that teen would forever bear the stigma of being the one asshole who didn't return what they took.

As Rudy opened the door, Angie took one last look around outside to see if anyone or anything might have seen them come this way. She was still greatly disturbed by the weird burning footprints, although she was more worried about the zombies at this point. She had no idea where Archie and his friends had gone. It was possible, she supposed, that they hadn't all escaped the fire at the café, which she could still see casting dancing light and shadows down the street. Even without the intervention of firefighters, she was certain by now that it wasn't going to spread, so at the very least they didn't need to worry about being overtaken by an inferno. At least not yet. If something happened again like in the café then she supposed that was still a possibility.

"Nobody turn on the lights," she said as they entered the museum.

"Then how the hell are we supposed to see in this maze?" Kevin asked.

"You mean you don't already know the layout by heart?" Jasmine asked. Kevin grunted something that might have been agreement. Still, even if all of them knew the layout by heart, it would be easy for someone to break their toe on some jutting display or artifact.

"I think they kept some flashlights by the cash register in case of emergencies," Rudy said. In the dim light coming through the glass door, the only window in the entire building, Angie saw him shuffling around behind a counter. On the walls around him were maps of Lake Superior, a few of them actually historical but most of them intended for tourists to buy. The largest and biggest seller was a map of most of the major shipwrecks recorded on the lake complete with little illustrations of each ship. That was the one all the tourists wanted because it included the *Edmund Fitzgerald*, even though that particular ship hadn't sunk anywhere near here. For the same reason, there was a small display of Gordon Lightfoot CDs next to the register so the vacationers could get that song stuck in their head on the long drive home.

"Here," Rudy said, producing three flashlights. Angie, Beth, and Jasmine all took one.

"Don't turn them on yet," Angie said. "We need to find something to cover up the glass door so none of the flashlights can be seen from outside.

They considered some of the maps for a moment but decided they were all too thin and wouldn't provide much cover. After some more scrounging around, they found some dusty black cloth that might have been used in some long ago display and then forgotten in a deep alcove under the counter. Trying to hang the cloth up over the door without any additional light was a struggle and in the end it didn't cover up the whole thing, leaving a thin sliver underneath where light would still be able to get through. Also, anyone on the outside who took too close of a look at the door would realize it had been covered, but Angie hoped none of the zombies maintained enough of their intelligence to figure that out.

"Okay, now you can turn them on," Angie said. "Try not to shine them anywhere near that gap at the bottom of the door."

The three flashlights turned on, illuminating the dark and cluttered museum. It was a museum only in the loosest definition of the word. Rather than being behind glass or on special display stands, most of the historical items were haphazardly placed on tables with old typewriter-written descriptions on cardboard cards denoting what they were and why they were supposed to be significant. Someone had at least made an effort to make sure that the tables were nicer, except for a few exhibits displayed on card tables that had been covered with cloth. The effect was less like a museum full of priceless historical artifacts and more like a garage sale hastily assembled in someone's barn.

The actual items on display ranged all the way from "Why is this even here?" to "Wow, that's really pretty cool." The museum consisted of three or four loosely organized rooms, if rooms could really be said to be made from partial sheets of painted plywood and curtains. Angie had been through it all on several occasions, sometimes because she was just bored and other times because she was genuinely curious about the town's eccentric history. An alcove near the front counter had floor-to-ceiling straining bookshelves, holding everything from hand-written accounts of ship's journeys over the Great Lakes to the town's old plat books for the last hundred and fifty years. One time in late high school she had got it in her head to find out what the name Mukwunaguk even meant but no two people could give her the same answer. The popular myth told to the tourists was that it was Ojibwe for "where the earth meets the waters." Upon actually inspecting deep into this stack of books, though, she had eventually found the original town hall meeting records where the original settlers came up with the name. They had literally just made up a word that, in the words of the town fathers themselves, "sounded like something from the savage tongue." It was a revelation so amusing that Angie had kept it to herself so she could smile inwardly whenever someone else spouted BS about the town's origins. Apparently Mukwunaguk meant "clueless white tourists will believe anything."

Farther along the next wall, the museum was dedicated to a series of displays and dioramas depicting the early life of settlers in the town, the clothes and dishes and cradles and knick-knacks dusty from years of the caretakers forgetting about them. The small dioramas on the tables were odd and amateurish, but they themselves were part of history, the creations of the original toothpick factory owner's wife as she'd convalesced from some never identified illness. The creepy little wooden dolls in the dioramas were a particular favorite of the teens to abscond with, and Angie herself had a particular fondness for the tiny baby figure in one of them that had a missing eye, her own personal prize when she had gone through that rite of passage when she was fourteen.

The back room consisted of the larger, more impressive, and occasionally just odd antiques and curiosities. The largest piece was an old Model-T, supposedly the first motor car ever in Mukwunaguk. Next to it were various small parts of a different Model-T, the one that was *supposed* to have been the first in town but had ended up in the lake when the ship it was on hit a previously unnoticed rock in the harbor. On the wall above the complete Model-T there hung the humungous lacquered cross section of a tree that had been cut down in the early days of logging in the area, a testament to the power of nature as well as the power of humans to ignore that power in the face of needing toothpicks. The propellers and several twisted pieces of metal from a plane crash in the Porcupine Mountains in the thirties were displayed on a wall in the corner right next to a rusty shovel. The shovel didn't look like much, but the yellowing card next to it marked it as the most macabre item in the whole museum, the weapon used in the only deliberate murder in Mukwunaguk's recorded history.

As she looked around at all this, though, Angie couldn't help but feel an unexpected tug at her heartstrings as her flashlight came around to the final section, the one that by design all the tourists came to last. Because, while everything else in the museum might have been nothing more than charming or peculiar curiosities, the real draw of Mukwunaguk was Lake Superior itself. Simply coming into the museum cost just a couple dollars, but the majority of the historical society's money was made with souvenirs and the lighthouse tour. And the lighthouse tour technically started right here.

This final section of the museum was dedicated to Superior and all its myths, legends, history, and folklore. This was where Old Bert, when he wasn't drowning himself at the Sand Bar or muttering to himself about all the outsiders, had plied his trade during the summer months. He would take up his typical spot next to the display of original mirrors from the lighthouse, the ones that had been replaced with less effective cosmetic ones for the tourists going into the tower once the lighthouse had no longer been in a proper position to accurately warn away ships. Irascible old curmudgeon that he'd been, Bert's eyes would light up and he'd become a different person when he started the tour. He'd talk about the history of shipping on the lake. He'd talk about Native American legends regarding its great waters (although she'd often suspected that actual Native Americans would take one listen to his stories and call bullshit on him for completely making most of them up). He'd gesture to the maps on the walls and point out the various artifacts around them that had been pulled out of the chilly deeps. And he'd always end with the story of the *Maltan*, a ship that had set sail from Minnesota in November of 1910, intending to make one last trip over the lake to Mukwunaguk itself before the harsh winter weather made Superior impassable. The ship had never arrived. He would show the tourists the only thing that *had* arrived, a silver cylinder with a single roll of paper inside. The cylinder was supposed to have had the ship's logs inside, but whoever had been in charge of maintaining such things hadn't done their job and all they'd managed to put inside was a single hastily written letter. Old Bert would open the cylinder, remove the letter, and read it out loud in a haunting voice that no one would have otherwise thought could come from him. It said goodbye to the crews' friends and family, and asked that God would have mercy on their souls.

By the time Bert had finished, all the tourists had been more than willing to fork over the cash to go on the next part of the tour.

Angie toyed with the cylinder in its typical place under the maps. As far as she was aware, most of that story was true, and the cylinder itself was the real deal, the last thing handled by dead men from over a century ago. The letter Old Bert had always pulled out from inside was fake, though, even if he did claim it was the exact words of the cylinder's actual final message. That particular piece of paper was long gone, handled by so many fingers that it had disintegrated to mulch long ago, but Old Bert had never admitted that to the tourists. To them, it had been real.

Occasional asshole or not, Angie almost felt there was something mystical about a person who could make others feel like that. And now Old Bert was gone, unceremoniously turned to ashes right along with so much else Angie had held dear throughout her life.

The complete and unreal horror of the night so far was only now dawning on her. A large part of Angie wanted to go curl up in the musty book alcove and go to sleep, hopefully to wake up soon and find that none of it had been real. But as she moved her flashlight over the faces of the others, all of them looking expectantly around at each other for someone to tell them what to do next, she realized she couldn't do that. The same thing that had made her keep going after her father had died came back to her now, an iron will and a healthy dose of stubbornness. She was the only leader these people had right now, and while they might have deserved better she still thought they could do much worse.

"Okay," she said to them all. "Let's figure out what to do next."

NINE

After a short deliberation among them all, it turned out that "what to do next" happened to not be much of anything all. It had been less than an hour and a half since the first one of the customers had walked into the café, but in that short time they'd been confronted by more than any of them could possibly deal with. They needed a moment to rest. Angie was fine with that. While they were resting they could talk, discuss, try to figure out what was happening. Johnny looked like he was in terrible shape and they needed to use this moment of quiet to try helping him. Megan, on the other hand, seemed to be slowly waking up. And once she was fully conscious and coherent, Angie hoped she could shed some light onto why their little town had apparently become the center of the zombie apocalypse.

With Old Bert gone, Rudy was the one who knew his way around the museum the best, and he and Jasmine led Johnny off to find the first aid kit. Kevin and Beth also promptly disappeared into a dark corner. To do what, Angie didn't think she really wanted to know, but if they were about to relieve some tension with each other, she didn't think she could blame them. It only seemed natural to her to think about love and sex in the face of death. She just said more power to them and hoped they would be discreet enough that no one else accidently walked in on them, wherever they might be going.

This left Angie, Boris, Kim, and Megan in the front near the register. Angie felt distinctly uncomfortable being so close to Boris with so few other people around. Thankfully, though, he didn't seem to be in the mood for any typical douchbaggery. Angie caught him looking at her more than once, but it wasn't with the naked lust he usually reserved for her. The expression was more complex and not entirely menacing. She almost thought it might partially be respect, but she wasn't going to assume. For all she knew, he could just be thinking of his next hackneyed attempt at a pickup line.

They'd sat Megan down on the floor with her back propped up against a table leg. When Angie shone the flashlight in her face, the girl blinked several times before closing her eyes and muttering something to herself. Angie took that to be a good sign. When she put the back of her hand against Megan's forehead, she found that the fever had gone down as well, although it was still noticeably there. It just wasn't at the point anymore where it didn't make any sense for her to be alive. Of course, for all Angie knew she really might be dead just like the four tourists still wandering the streets, although if she was then she was faking breathing very well.

"She's going to be okay, right?" Kim asked.

"Sure," Angie said, although she didn't think she sounded very convincing. The mark on Megan's neck and shoulder was still there, neither getting worse nor getting better. When Angie shone the light on the blackened flesh, flesh that for all intents and purposes should have required major medical attention, she couldn't help but be reminded of what she and Kevin had seen. Would he tell Beth about that while they were alone, she wondered? Probably not. It would spoil the mood. He probably didn't even want to think about it right now. Angie, on the other hand, didn't think she had the luxury of ignoring it. It was another piece of a puzzle she needed to solve if she wanted to keep anyone else from dying tonight.

"Kim, do you have any idea what Megan was doing this afternoon? Maybe where she might have gone?"

Kim sniffed. "She doesn't tell me much about what she does anymore. She's punishing me."

"Punishing you? For what?"

"For trying to raise her right."

While Angie highly doubted that, she wasn't sure whether she should push this or not. It was possible that there might be something along this line of questioning that would lead to an answer.

"What exactly do you mean by that?" Angie asked. She shot Boris a look that clearly said he needed to hold his tongue right now, even though it was obvious he wanted to say something rude to the woman.

"I made sure she was a good strong young woman," Kim said. "Me, and no one else. She resents that."

Angie nodded as though that made any sense at all.

"I've taught her that the world is always out to get her. And she knew it for a time. But then she started believing all the world's lies. Do you believe she actually told me once she believes that foolishness about people actually going to the moon? How gullible do you have to be?"

It took every ounce of Angie's strength to keep a straight face, but if Kim so much as uttered the word "sheeple" she thought she might lose it.

Kim, in a rare moment of clarity, seemed to realize she might be losing her audience and some of the outrage that had been growing in her voice diminished. "I know that other people think there's something wrong with me. But I know better. All I've ever tried to do is what was best for my child. You can understand that, right?"

For a moment, Angie almost felt sympathy for Kim. Then she remembered back to middle school and the way Megan had been, so shy, so fragile-looking, almost like she was afraid her own shadow would drunkenly accuse the next person that walked by of being the true culprit behind the Kennedy assassination. That was what Kim had done to her daughter despite her best intentions.

Angie realized she was gently stroking Megan's hand in her own and let go. The girl still wasn't fully conscious. That most definitely wasn't appropriate and Angie felt ashamed of herself. Yet even as she looked at Megan's face, she remembered back to that girl that she had always wanted to protect from the bullies. Maybe, now that she was publicly admitting to the world the true nature of who she was attracted to, she could admit to herself that the protectiveness of those early years had been the result of a little crush. She doubted Megan would feel the same way, though.

"Let's get back to focusing on the issue at hand, Kim," Angie said. "Any clue at all about what she might have been doing earlier? Even the slightest thing might be helpful."

Kim looked down and her thin hands in her lap. There was a sound coming from the back of her throat, barely audible, that sounded like a suppressed cry of anguish. Or maybe anger.

"Kim, you do know something, don't you?"

"Yes."

"And?"

"And I don't want to say it. It makes me ashamed."

"Ashamed of what? Of something you did?"

Kim's head jerked up so she could look Angie in the eyes. Something about the defiantness of her stare made Angie uneasy.

"No. I haven't done anything wrong. I never did anything wrong. It was always other people blaming me."

Angie didn't respond, hoping Kim would continue without getting too much more agitated.

"Ashamed of her," Kim finally said, nodding toward her daughter.

Angie leaned forward. "Why? What did she do?"

Kim took a deep breath, as though she were about to reveal one of the darkest secrets of the universe. "She went into the pharmacy."

Angie had to fight not to show her disappointment. So much for Kim being able to give important information.

"Why is that so bad?" Boris asked. Angie would have asked him not to if there had been some way to do it without Kim seeing. Boris had spent a lot of time here growing up, but that was mostly in the summers when his family had come around to run one of the souvenir shops. He hadn't become a more permanent resident until later. He probably wasn't already intimately acquainted with what was about to spew out of Kim's mouth.

"Because that means she's putting chemicals into her body!" The words came out of Kim's mouth as just short of a scream. Angie made a shushing gesture and the next thing Kim said was quieter, but not by much. "I've been saying her whole life how dangerous that crap is, how it wrecks the brain and keeps us from our true potential."

This, at least, prompted Boris to give Angie a raised eyebrow. Even if he didn't know about her well-known phobia of pharmaceuticals, he at least knew her reputation around a bottle. If Old Bert had been known to tip back a few once in a while, he had at least been known to stay semi-functional. Kim, on the other hand, couldn't always say that.

Kim smoothed Megan's hair gently with her hand, although now the gesture seemed less motherly and more creepy. "But I can get her back. I know I can."

Angie thought of that pill bottle that had fallen out of Megan's pocket earlier. She surreptitiously checked the pocket again, feeling the outside to be sure it was still there without Kim hopefully realizing it. There was a reason Megan needed it, after all, and she didn't want Kim to find it and throw it away when no one was looking.

Assuming Megan still needed any medication at all after tonight. That would require her to remain alive right along with the rest of them.

Deciding that this line of questioning wouldn't do her any good until Megan was again capable of speaking for herself, Angie stood up and went to find Johnny, Rudy, and Jasmine. Boris followed her.

"Just watch your hands in the dark, buddy," she said. "I feel them touching anything they shouldn't and they'll become the next display in a pickle jar."

"Jesus, I'm not going to touch you without your permission," Boris said. "I'm starting to think you have the wrong idea about me."

"Oh really? So that wasn't pickup artist techniques you were trying on me earlier? What, did you just accidentally read *The Game* and think doing those things would make you just a generally more likeable person?"

She turned her flashlight on him to see that he was blushing. Apparently, she'd struck a nerve. "I'm sorry," he said. "Maybe that wasn't the right thing to do."

"Oh no, using techniques designed to lower a woman's self-esteem just so she'll sleep with you is *definitely* the moral thing to do. I see it now. How could I have been so blind?"

Boris sighed. "Look. I'm sorry. I just didn't know what else to do to make you into me."

"You can't *make* someone fall madly in love with someone else. Or just make them desperately want to have sex with you, if that's all you're really wanting from me. Is it?"

"Well, um…" He didn't say anything else. That was all the

answer she needed.

"Instead of playing mind games you found on the internet, did it ever occur to you just once that the best way to approach me about casual sex might be to just ask me?"

He looked surprised. "Would that work?"

"You're never going to know unless you try."

"So, uh, you ever think about having sex with me?"

"Oh hell no."

He frowned. "And that's why I didn't ask that way originally."

"News flash. It was never going to happen one way or the other. I'm just not into you. But you would have saved yourself a lot of embarrassment if you had just acted like a decent human about it from the beginning."

He stopped and let her go the rest of the way through the museum until she got to one of the back storage rooms. From the sounds coming from behind the thin wall nearby, Kevin and Beth were enjoying their alone time together but at least doing everyone else the courtesy of trying to keep it down. Neither Johnny, Jasmine, nor Rudy seemed to hear it, or if they did they pretended not to.

"So, how's it looking?" Angie asked them.

"I don't feel so hot," Johnny said. Angie wondered for a moment if that had been an intentional pun, given what they had all just witnessed, but he didn't appear to have the energy left for even that lame attempt at humor.

"I pulled out what pieces of glass I could," Jasmine said. "And I found this gauze to wrap around his face as much as possible. But he needs stitches."

Angie shook her head. "He's probably not going to get them. Even if we find a way out of all this and we somehow get someone on the outside to believe us, there's a time limit on how long there can be between a cut and getting stitches. We wouldn't be able to get him to a hospital on time."

"Has anyone thought to try calling emergency services?" Rudy asked.

"Um, Rudy?" Angie asked. "Don't you remember? You did."

"Okay, but that was just the local dispatch. We've all got cell phones here, don't we? Has anyone tried calling someone outside of town?"

It was such a simple idea that Angie was ashamed it hadn't occurred to her earlier, but at least she wasn't alone in her boneheaded moment. She pulled her smart phone out of her coat pocket and went through her list of contacts. The problem was she didn't know too many people that lived outside of town. She supposed she could try 411. Or maybe there was a phone book somewhere around here with additional emergency numbers outside of town.

After a couple of seconds of fiddling with the phone, though, she realized something was missing. "I don't have any bars."

"Really?" Jasmine asked. "I didn't think the museum was in one of the dead spots." She patted herself down, looking for her own phone, then shook her head. "I must have left it in the diner."

"Don't look at me, I've never owned one of those damned things in the first place," Rudy said. "Never saw the point."

"I don't know, Rudy," Angie said. "I kind of see the point right now, don't you?"

Rudy grinned sheepishly. "I suppose. What about you?" he asked Johnny. "You've got to have one on you, right?"

He didn't. Johnny had also left it behind to burn up in the fire. Angie didn't think that would be too much of a problem, though. With nine other people in the building, at least one of them had to have a cell phone that worked.

She went to ask Boris, who glumly told her that he'd left his at home in the charger. Once she thought Kevin and Beth might be finished, she politely knocked on the door of the broom closet they'd hidden in and asked if either of them had one. Beth did, which she handed out the door and then closed it before Angie could get any idea what state of dress either of them might be in. It didn't do any good, however, since Beth's phone wasn't getting a signal either. She finally checked Meghan's phone. Nothing. It wasn't just a matter of individual phones not being powerful enough, and they should have been in a part of town where they could all receive a signal. If they couldn't get the signal, that meant there was no signal at all.

"But I don't understand. How can there not be a signal?" Kevin asked. He was walking up to the rest of the group, which had convened again near the register. Beth was right next to him, looking for all the world in the dim flashlight beams like she had just spent hours in front of a mirror, all her hair and makeup completely in place. The only sign that she might have been up to something was the thin sheen of sweat on her forehead, an interesting feat considering the entire building was at the lowest temperature it could go without freezing. Kevin, on the other hand, had his shirt half tucked in and half out of his pants, which were only zipped part way up. He apparently realized this as he approached, hiding his crotch behind one of the tables just long enough to zip the rest of the way. His words came out labored as he was still trying to catch his breath from something. Angie looked at Beth, who gave her a shrug and a peculiar half smile that seemed to say, "My secret techniques are my own. Don't ask for them."

"If you had blood going to your brain rather than other body parts right now, maybe you'd figure it out," Rudy said. "It's the cell tower. Something must be wrong with it."

"But cell towers don't just fail," Beth said.

"They do if someone sabotages them somehow," Angie replied.

"Are you implying that the zombies are deliberately cutting off communication?" Boris asked. "They can't do that. They don't have the intelligence."

"We need to stop making assumptions about what zombies can and can't do," Angie said. "Just because George Romero made a movie in the sixties and everybody copied him without using their own imaginations doesn't mean that's how it's going to work in real life."

Boris snorted. "And yet somehow they know traditional zombie dance moves."

Jasmine nodded. "You noticed that too? I thought I was just seeing things."

"Maybe we're just relying too much on modern technology," Johnny said. While his words were still sluggish, especially since his face was covered in bandages, he gave every impression that he might be stable for the moment. "Even if someone somehow took out the cell tower, there's still landlines, right? Especially in a place like this that hasn't really been updated for the twenty-first century."

Angie started to look around for a telephone but Rudy stopped her. "They disconnect the telephone service here during the off season. Maybe if we were in another building, we might be able to get something."

She was noncommittal about that. Sure, maybe they could, but she had to wonder. If someone or something was capable of taking out a freaking cell tower somehow, then it seemed in the realm of possibility that they would also have thought about the land lines. Which only led right back to the question of who could possibly do this.

Kevin seemed to have the same thought, as that look of post-coital bliss on his face instantly disappeared. "Think we should tell them?"

Everyone stared at them both.

"Well, kind of have to now, don't we?" Angie said. "We can't exactly hide the fact we have a secret when you've just admitted to everyone."

"Oh. Uh, right."

"Well?" Boris asked. "Are you going to tell us or not?"

"Is this about whatever you saw with the dog?" Jasmine asked.

"I don't get why you're so reluctant to tell us," Rudy said. "It's not like anything you saw could have possibly been crazier than zombies."

Angie and Kevin let those words hang in the air.

"Oh Christ," Rudy muttered to himself.

"Please just end the suspense and tell us what you saw," Jasmine said.

"I'm not even sure what we saw," Kevin said. The two of them took turns giving details of the footprints trailing away over the sidewalk, footprints that were both strangely human and not at the same time, footprints so hot they could damage concrete. When they finished, no one spoke for a long time.

"Okay," Boris finally said. "Under normal circumstances, I would try saying there was some kind of scientific explanation for what you saw. Except I'm just going to skip that step for now. Because, you know, zombies and everything already. Why the hell not add burning footprints from Hell?"

"Is that what you think they were?" Jasmine asked with a raised eyebrow.

"I don't know what to think, but sure. Why the hell not?"

"As in, like a demon or something?" Johnny asked. "I don't know I can believe that."

Beth shrugged at him. "And I don't know that I can believe in zombie tourists doing dance moves from old 80s videos right before they burst into flames."

"Point taken," Johnny said.

"We can't make assumptions, though," Angie said. "We have no way of knowing for sure if whatever caused the footprints has anything to do with the zombies."

"Angie, this may be a town where we believe we have haunted lighthouses and lake monsters," Rudy said, "but it's not like this is a town at the center of the Twilight Zone. If two separate horrible and bizarre things are happening at the same time, they're probably related."

"A demon, though?" Boris asked. "Years of pop culture have prepared me for the acceptance of zombies, but I'm not sure if I'm ready to mix that up with demons. Too many subgenres at once."

"…not…demon."

The words were so faint that they were almost lost in their intense conversation. It took Angie a few seconds to realize they hadn't come from any of the people who had already been speaking, but were in fact coming from closer to her feet. Angie shone her flashlight down at Megan and Kim to see that Megan's eyes were open, even if they were still unfocused and blurry. Angie kneeled down next to her and put her ear close so Megan wouldn't have to strain herself.

"What was that, Megan?"

"Not a demon."

"What's not a demon?"

"Not, uh, really. Don't think so."

"Megan, this is important. If there's anything you know, you need to tell us. It could be the only thing that could keep us alive."

"So sleepy, though."

"Yes, I know. But this is important. Please. What happened to you? Where were you? How did this happen?"

"Need to rest some more…" Her voice trailed off. Unconsciousness was obviously close again.

"Megan, please. Anything you can give us. Anything at all."

Megan muttered something incoherent, then the words stopped. Just to be sure, Angie checked that Megan was still breathing. She was, and at a much more normal pace than she had been earlier in the café. Her skin temperature was about the same, though. A quick check of her wound showed that it was leaking puss which, while disgusting, might have actually been a good sign. That might mean it was healing. Of course, Angie didn't think it was possible for this kind of grievous wound to heal that quickly. Megan still looked like she would make it through the night, providing of course that the rest of them did as well. Angie didn't think she would be getting any more info out of her for the time being, though.

"She," Beth said. "Whoever did this to her was a woman."

That wasn't enough information for them to learn anything, but something else had been tickling at the far corners of her mind. Angie thought back to the recording they had found on the phone. She didn't know off the top of her head how long a phone would keep recording video if left to its own devices, but she remembered that it hadn't still been recording when she'd pulled it out of Megan's pocket. Megan had accidentally started recording when she'd put it in, but what had caused it to stop? Either she had bumped it in just the right way again, or…

"Someone turned it off," Angie whispered.

"What was that?" Jasmine asked.

"Her phone. It was recording in her pocket, but it wasn't recording when we took it out to look at it. Someone turned it off."

"Maybe it was just Megan, though," Johnny said.

"Why would she think to turn the recording off if she didn't even know it was on?" Kevin asked.

Angie pulled out Megan's phone again and looked at it. This time she didn't care whether or not it had any bars. She went back to the video it had captured earlier.

"Please don't make us listen to that again," Kim said.

"Don't you guys see?" Angie asked. "We never finished it. None of us wanted to keep listening to that scream so we turned it off. But the video wasn't over yet!"

She started the video again. As before, the picture gave them nothing useful, but they listened even more carefully than earlier to the muttering in the audio. Angie still couldn't make out what was being said, but she let it keep going even as Megan's awful scream reverberated through the museum. Once it cut off, though, Angie let the video keep going. Everyone moved in closer to see if the tiny screen showed anything new. For several seconds, it didn't. All sound from the phone cut off and Angie thought maybe that really was the end of the video after all. Then the picture moved.

The blurry view of the inside of Megan's pocket turned gray, the color the sky had been that afternoon. The waves of Lake Superior, previously hushed by the fabric of Megan's coat, were now clearly audible. There was the sound of fumbling as someone moved the phone around. Angie prepared herself to see something vital any second, but the camera stayed pointed up, directly at the sky. They obviously weren't going to get anything useful out of the video after all. The audio, on the other hand…

"Hello," a voice said through the phone. It was raw and scratchy, similar to what Angie's sounded like after a night of nervous chain smoking, but it was at least clear enough that they could all tell it belonged to a woman. "If things have gone as I've foreseen, and there's no reason to think they haven't, then the person currently holding this phone should be Angela Zwiersky."

Angie dropped the phone like it had burned her. She looked up at the others, hoping they hadn't heard the same thing she had. From the looks on their faces, however, it hadn't been some kind of auditory hallucination. The person who had held this phone hours earlier had very clearly called her by name.

The voice chuckled, a strangely ugly sound that somehow managed to evoke the noise of two pieces of coal being rubbed together vigorously. "Go ahead and debate this turn of events among yourself for a few seconds. I'll wait for you to pick the phone back up."

"Holy shit," Kevin said. "No way."

"Turn it off," Kim said. Angie would have expected her to sound panicked at this point, but her voice was oddly calm, as though this kind of bizarre thing happened to her all the time. Who knew, Angie thought. In Kim's mind, maybe it did. "Just turn it off so we don't have to listen to it."

"Let me just interject and say you're not going to turn it off," the recording said. "I've seen that much, as well."

"This can't be happening," Johnny said. "There's no way."

"Maybe we *should* turn it off," Jasmine said. "Especially if whoever that is thinks we won't."

"I don't think we should," Angie said. "I think we might need to hear whatever she has to say. Maybe she has some answers."

"Oh, I do," the recording said.

"Stop that!" Beth said. Angie expected the recording to say something in response. It would have been the perfect chance to taunt them, after all. Yet the voice ignored that golden opportunity.

"I don't think we really have much choice but to keep listening," Angie said.

"And since all of you have followed Zwiersky around so blindly all evening, I know this is the point where I can now start explaining again," the recording said. "Not that I actually intend to explain everything. That would rob me of my spectacular moment later."

"I, uh, if we ask you questions right now, will you respond?" Angie asked.

"If I so choose. Then again, maybe I won't. It's much more fun sometimes to keep you all guessing."

"This can't be happening," Johnny muttered. "There's no way."

"Since little Miss Howzer is quite incapable of telling you much of anything anymore, let me describe to you what is going to happen next." The voice paused. "Or what happened hours ago, according to your perspective.

"I am going to release Megan Howzer in her current disoriented state back into the town proper. She'll drive along as best as she can manage for a while before she crashes into light pole in front of the Gitchigumi Café. Zwiersky and Boris Romanoff will bring her in where everyone will fret over her for a while before everything starts to go crazy. How close am I so far?"

"Way too close," Angie muttered.

"This has to be some kind of trick," Johnny said. "Someone must have planted this message on the phone after all that happened."

"That doesn't seem likely," Beth said.

"Now really, does that sound at all likely to you?" the recording said. Beth looked puzzled at that. Angie, on the other hand, thought maybe she was beginning to see a pattern. "Now here's what else will happen. As soon as I send Howzer on her way, I'm going to head into this nearby cabin and do the same thing to the tourists there that I just did to her. And then they will spread their infection to the sheriff and his partner and everyone else who arrives to answer the 911 call that the tourists are placing at the very moment I say this. Then all of them will head into town. They will bite and infect others. By morning, there will be one person left alive. Only one out of all of you huddling right there in the Mukwunaguk Historical Society Museum. Everyone else among you will be dead, either infected with my plague or burned to a crisp like the two in the café."

Bingo. Angie instantly understood something, but as she looked at the faces of the others they didn't seem to catch it. They were too busy being terrified by the supernatural voice predicting their fate.

"Who are you?" Boris asked the phone. "Why are you doing this? Or even how?"

The voice sighed. "Unfortunately, there are certain, oh, let's call them forces higher than myself, that specifically stated that they want my influence to be minimal in this. I simply proposed that I would do my job here and deliver a zombie infection. I said it would be in the traditional vein, but that definition isn't as clear cut as some would believe. I added in a few so-called 'traditional' elements that amused me."

Such as zombies that moved suspiciously like Michael Jackson, Angie thought, but she didn't say it out loud.

"That still doesn't give us any answers," Rudy muttered.

"Too bad, because that's all you get. For now at least. I'll monologue a bit about everything when you finally come face to face with me just before dawn. I know I won't be able to resist. The two of you that will be left at that point will hang on my every word, I'm sure."

"She's got to be trying to psych us out," Boris said. "There's no way she can know who's going to die and who's going to survive."

The recording laughed. "You really haven't gotten a clue yet just what or who I am yet, have you? Or maybe you have a guess, but it's probably wrong. Suffice it to say, I'm old. I'm powerful. And the Hell you are all experiencing tonight is just me practicing for what I will unleash in the future. So a little bit of clairvoyance to find out which of you aren't going to make it isn't hard. Hell, it's not even the hardest thing I've done in the last five minutes."

"Actually, I don't think she's as all-seeing as she says she is," Angie said. "And I'm proving it right now with the fact that she doesn't know that I'm talking."

"Oh, I wouldn't say that," the recording said. For a moment, Angie thought she had been wrong, that the mistake had been on her part rather than on the mysterious voice, but then it continued. "You can rage against me all you like, Kevin, but it's not going to change anything."

"Uh, I didn't say anything," Kevin said.

"Fine, since you all still don't believe me, I'll tell you exactly what's going to happen next. Once this recording shuts off, Angela will turn on this phone's stopwatch function. When it hits exactly thirty minutes and thirty nine seconds, you will be out of time to plan what you're going to do next. Because that's when one of the zombies I have roaming the streets will see a flash of light from your location and get the attention of all the others. Most of you will go on to the place of your final stand. Two of you will not. Sorry Kevin. Sorry Johnny.

"Oh, look at that. It looks like my little infection is starting to work its magic on Miss Megan. It's about time I sent her running on along to you now.

"I will see some of you soon. I'm sure it will be entertaining."

The recording ended.

TEN

As much as it loathed Angie to play into the mysterious voice's expectations, the first thing she did was find the stopwatch tool on Megan's phone and start it. There were a great many things the woman might have lied about and a few things Angie knew she got outright wrong, but if there was any truth at all to the amount of time they had then she wanted to be ready.

"I do apologize if I smell, everyone," Kevin said.

"Why's that?" Boris asked.

"Because I think I might have just shit myself in fear." Beth looked at the seat of his pants just to make sure he was joking. At this point, Angie wouldn't blame him if he actually had.

"This is insane," Jasmine said.

"We've got to get out of here," Johnny said. "We can't stay. The zombies can't find us here in thirty minutes if we aren't actually here."

"Just calm down," Angie said. "For all we know that could have been a ploy to get us to leave early and get us all killed."

"Does it even matter?" Rudy asked, his tone more defeatist than anything Angie had ever heard from him. "You heard everything that woman said. Whoever she is, she can predict everything we're going to do. There's no way to escape it. Only one of us is going to live through the night."

"Actually I don't think that's true," Angie said. "However she's doing this and whatever the reason, somewhere along the line she made a mistake."

"Yeah, you said something like that a minute ago," Beth said. "What did you mean?"

"Didn't you all hear? The conversation wasn't as perfectly synchronized as she thought it would be. Kevin, that bit at the end where she responded to something you didn't say? I'm betting that was where you were supposed to scream at her or threaten her or something."

"And why would I have done that?" Kevin asked.

"Because you were supposed to be angry at her." Angie took a deep breath, partially because she wanted to ground herself from getting too excited at the idea that they might have a way out of this. Also, though, it was for dramatic effect. "For the death of your wife."

Beth raised her eyebrows. "Say what now?"

"You might have all been too shocked by what was going on that you missed it, but I didn't. She said two people died in the fire, yet the only one who didn't make it out was Bert. And every time Beth spoke, she acted like no one had said anything at all. According to our mystery woman's visions, Beth isn't supposed to be here anymore. And because she was wrong about that, we might have an opportunity to make her wrong about the rest of it, as well."

"But how is that possible?" Jasmine asked. "She sounded so sure about everything."

"I think maybe her miscalculation is right here," Angie said. She put a hand against Megan's forehead again. Sure enough she thought the fever might be breaking, and Megan reacted slightly to her touch.

"I don't understand any of this," Kim said. She'd been silent through the entire phone conversation. She hadn't even looked like she'd been paying that much attention, instead holding Megan's hand as she murmured in her sleep.

"I'm not quite following it either," Johnny said.

"No, I think I get it," Boris said. He smiled at Angie. She was mildly surprised that the expression managed not to be creepy. "Beth was supposed to die because we weren't supposed to be attacked by five zombies. We were supposed to be attacked by six."

"You mean Megan herself?" Jasmine asked.

"Yes," Angie said. "We were all afraid that she was going to turn into a zombie like the others. Well, I think she was supposed to. But she didn't. Something happened that this woman couldn't predict."

"Okay, but where's the difference?" Beth asked. "What happened that changed everything the woman saw was going to happen?"

Angie shrugged. "I don't know. We might have to wait for Megan to be able to tell us. Or maybe Megan just won't know. All that's important is some kind of butterfly effect thing happened, so our dooms aren't as certain as that woman said they are. We can still get out of this."

Jasmine gestured at the clothed-over front door. "We can, but what about everyone else in town? They can't all have been gotten by the zombies yet."

Angie hesitated. "I...don't know if there's anything we can do for anyone else."

"But we've got to try, don't we?" Jasmine asked. "I've known these people my entire life. I can't just let them die. Even the ones that are assholes."

Angie shook her head, thinking of who else might be out there. Luke, the first boy she had ever kissed before he dumped her for a mathlete. Jenna, the Sunday school teacher who used to come into the café late on Sunday mornings. Despite being older than Angie by about ten years, Angie's thoughts about Jenna late at night had been among the early indications she was something other than completely straight. Every single person who permanently lived in the town during the winter was a regular customer of hers at the café. She said hi to them on the street. She occasionally shared beers with them at the Sand Bar. There was a group of people, not exactly friends but closer than just casual relations, that she would sometimes play Euchre with on Thursday nights. Was she really prepared to accept that they were all dead or at least about to be?

There were a couple hundred of them. As much as it hurt her heart, she couldn't save them all. She did have a chance, however, to save the eight other people around her.

"We can't just run around the town willy-nilly checking everyone's homes. Mukwunaguk may be small, but not small enough that we can do that without attracting whatever horde has gathered by now. And yes, despite any earlier arguments, I'm sure there would be enough zombies by now to be called a horde by any definition."

Megan stirred and murmured. Her eyelids fluttered. Maybe she was about to wake up for real this time. Angie pointed at her. "If she is indeed some kind of x-factor that whoever was on the phone didn't account for, then we have a real chance, just us, of surviving."

"I don't know if I'm ready to just let my friends die," Boris said.

"You have friends?" Kevin asked.

"Screw you."

"They're probably already dead, Boris. Or about to be. Soon enough that we won't be able to do anything about it."

Boris sighed. "Okay. So now what?"

"We have to get out of town," Rudy said. "If we can't call out, we need to at least get to somewhere else and warn everyone."

"And how do you propose doing that?" Beth asked. "We sent Becca to go get a car, and we know what happened there."

"We don't need to get a vehicle," Angie said. "We already have one, and it's even big enough to fit all of us comfortably."

"What do you mean?" Kevin asked.

"Oh," Jasmine said. "I get it."

"So do I," Rudy said.

"Care to clue in the rest of us?" Boris asked.

"We passed our way out on the way in, actually," Angie said. "In the garage out back."

"The tour bus," Johnny said.

"Do any of us even know how to drive that thing?" Beth asked.

"I might be able to," Rudy said. "I hung around Bert enough to watch him do it. Not much different than driving a truck, really."

"But where would we even go with it?" Jasmine asked.

"Does that even matter?" Kevin asked. "We get out of town. Away from the zombies. The nearest place with a phone, anywhere."

"I've got an even better question," Beth asked. "How are we supposed to get it going? I mean, it's not like any of just happen to have a set of keys to a random tour bus in our purses."

"Old Bert would have," Johnny muttered.

"Maybe we can start the tour bus the same way we got in here," Angie said. "They must have kept a second set of keys around here, right?"

No one needed any more instruction after that. For the next fifteen minutes, every able-person in the group frantically searched the museum for a second set of keys. Kim even got up and did some searching, although she tended to search highly unlikely places like the dioramas. Once or twice, Angie went over to check on Megan and saw that she was coming around. She was awake but groggy enough that she couldn't give Angie anything more than the occasional yes or no answers. As much as Angie wanted to stop and take a moment to question her more deeply, she knew they didn't have time. As they looked for the keys, the smartphone kept counting. Getting closer and closer to that thirty-minute mark.

To everyone's surprise, Kim was the one who actually found the keys. While everyone else searched the front counter or the back office or even the janitor's closet, Kim had continued poking around the displays themselves. When she finally called out that she saw them everyone converged around her. She sat in the front seat of the Model-T, pointing at something by the passenger's side.

The keys were sitting in the open glove compartment.

Johnny scratched his head. "Uh, do Model-Ts even have a glove compartment?" he asked.

"Apparently this one does," Kevin said.

"But why?" Beth asked.

Angie handed Megan's phone to Jasmine then gently pulled Kim out of the driver's seat, moving in for a closer look. The "glove compartment" was actually just a metal box that had been bolted into the car. Whoever had made it had taken great care to use similar materials and make it look aged, although the bolts that held it on were obviously newer. The average person who didn't know it wasn't supposed to be there would have assumed it was just a part of the car.

"Clever," Angie said. "Although I kind of doubt that's the sort of thing anyone would be able to get away with at any other museum."

The ring inside the compartment held far more keys than she thought were needed just for the museum. One was obviously a copy of the key to the museum itself. There were multiple others that she couldn't be sure of, at first, until she realized these were just the keys for here. This must have been an emergency key ring of entire historical society, including every place that they took care of throughout town. There were other historical sites and offices, after all. She thought for a moment that it wasn't so smart to place them in a building where it was a local tradition for people to just walk off with random things, but given that it was also tradition that everyone brought them back she supposed security wasn't their greatest concern.

Angie fingered through the keys, ignoring anything that was clearly supposed to be for a building until she found one that looked like it belonged to a vehicle. That would be the tour bus key.

"Great," she said. "How are we looking on time?" She looked to Jasmine, who held up the phone for all to see. They still had just under five minutes.

"Okay, we can do this. We know what causes the zombies to find us. Light. So everyone turn off their flashlights."

"That's going to lead to a lot of barked shins," Boris said.

"You can stub your toe or you can get your brain eaten," Angie said. "Weigh the options and make your decision." Angie thought for a second. The mystery voice would never have told them what would give them away if that knowledge could prevent it. They had to add in another factor. "Give all the flashlights to Beth. She's not supposed to be here, so maybe that will be enough to change things."

Beth accepted all the flashlights from them. In the complete dark, even with their eyes adjusting, it was hard to see any expression on Beth's face. But after a moment of hesitation unscrewed the caps of each flashlight and removed the batteries, putting them in a pocket well away from the flashlights. Smart, Angie thought.

"Good. Okay. Let's find the back door and quietly make our way out to the garage," Angie said. "Megan? Are you okay to walk yet?"

"I...huh?" Megan fumbled around as she awkwardly got to her feet. Something thumped as it fell on the floor, a heavy glass object from one of the displays that thankfully didn't break. "Where? Am I?"

"Better than nothing," Angie muttered. "Rudy and Jasmine, you want to stay on either side of her and steady her?"

Jasmine handed Megan's phone back to Angie, and as the clock counted up from its current twenty-seven minutes, Angie turned it off. There had to be no light. None at all. She thought about the rest of the museum around them, trying to think of anything that could make that deadly flash of light. There were the overhead lights, of course, but those were closer to the front than they were now, and Angie had already instinctively herded her group away from them. There was her lighter in her pocket, but as long as she didn't feel an uncontrollable urge to light up in the next couple minutes, that wouldn't be a problem. Of course, in that patented way that nic fits seemed to have, the mere thought of cigarettes was enough to make her desperately want one. It was an urge she could ignore.

"Alright, back door," Angie said again.

"I can't even see where it is," Kim mumbled.

"Through the office," Rudy said.

"One last roll call," Angie said, realizing she sounded suspiciously like the adult chaperones who would occasionally bring groups of kids through here. "Everyone here and ready?"

Everyone said they were ready, although Angie noticed one voice missing. "Johnny?"

"Over here," his voice coming from near the front cash register. Very close, Angie realized, to the light switches. "I just thought it might be a good idea if we had one of the maps in case we need to go too far from…"

"Don't move!" Angie called. The entire museum went quiet for a few seconds. Then she said, "Where are you?"

"Um…"

"Doesn't matter! Just do. Not. Move." She'd turned off the phone, so she had no idea exactly how much time had passed. Had the moment the voice predicted already come and gone, or was it going to happen any second now? And how did they know the voice hadn't been lying about when exactly it would happen? It might be a good idea for all of them to just stand here in complete silence for several minutes until they were positive the predicted moment had passed. Of course, that might have just been a ruse to ensure they were sitting ducks when the zombies did come.

"Are you anywhere near the light switches?" Angie asked.

Even from across the floor Angie could hear his audible gulp as he realized what she was afraid of. "Uh, yes. I think they're, like, a foot away from me."

"Okay. Step away from them. Slowly. Navigate your way through the displays as best you can until you reach…"

She heard all the sounds with perfect clarity. A thunk as his foot hit a table leg. Something small toppled over onto something larger, which in turn hit something that caused a creak and scrape, the sound of something large and glass as it tipped over from it place in a display.

The old lighthouse mirrors.

Johnny yelped as the mirror hit the floor and smashed behind him. Shards of glass flew everywhere, although Johnny managed to duck the worst of them this time. Angie could sort of see this because each tiny shard was sparkling, reflecting light from the small sliver of exposed glass at the bottom of the front door.

If the phone had still been on, Angie suspected it would currently read thirty minutes and thirty-nine seconds exactly.

"Run! Everyone to the back door!" Angie screamed. Keeping quiet no longer seemed particularly important. She heard shouts and thumps around her as people jarred the displays and one another in their desperate rush to reach the back office. It no longer seemed like such a great idea to have removed the batteries from the flashlights.

"I'm sorry! I'm sorry! I'm sorry!" Johnny said as he stumbled up next to them. Angie didn't particularly blame him, since it had been a mistake none of them had predicted.

"Maybe that wasn't it," Kevin said. "Maybe the zombies didn't see…"

There was a heavy thump at the front door, like someone's fist hammering against the glass. Angie thought she'd heard the glass crack, but she couldn't be sure from here.

Johnny and Kevin, Angie thought. Those were the ones who were supposed to die now. If she could keep them alive specifically, maybe she might be able to change everything else as well.

Rudy reached the back office and turned on the light, no longer bothering with trying to stay hidden. For at least a couple of seconds that proved to be a mistake, as all of them flinched at the sudden intrusion of brightness and slowed down. Two more thumps hit the glass up front with differing amounts of force, making Angie think there was no longer just one zombie there. The glass groaned, obviously ready to give way with just a little more provocation. Everyone piled into the small, cramped office and struggled to get around the administrator's desk to the emergency exit on the other side.

"Rudy, you have the keys. Keep them ready so we can get into the garage and then the bus ASAP," Angie said. "Johnny and Kevin, you two go out the door first. I want you as far away as possible when those zombies get in."

Rudy nodded, making sure the keys were ready in his hand. Johnny pushed through the others so he was right at the door. Kevin, sounding slightly out of breath, trailed behind.

Before Angie could give any more orders, Johnny opened the door. Immediately, a zombie hand reached through and grabbed his hair. Johnny screamed and tried to pull back, yanking the zombie that had him inside just enough for Angie to see that it was Louis, the town deputy. A second pair of zombie hands scrambled through the crack in the door, the fingers grasping at the air as though they thought there was supposed to be something there and were confused by its absence.

"Pull him in! Pull him in!" Angie screamed. Johnny screamed right along with her, a scream that only grew more frantic as Louis's mouth came down on his arm. Rudy and Kevin tried pulling him away from the door, but the second pair of hands stopped searching for their own target and instead grabbed his shirt.

As Louis took a bite out of Johnny's arm, Angie saw the spot immediately begin to smoke, the flesh around where Louis's lips latched, instantly blackening as though his arm had been shoved into a roaring fire. He let go with his teeth to grab Johnny with a firmer hold, and then yanked. Johnny fell out the door. Rudy didn't hesitate to pull the door closed behind him.

"What are you doing?" Kevin yelled. "We could still have got him!"

"No, kid, we couldn't," Rudy said. Kevin looked at him with horror for a few seconds before the truth dawned on him. Rudy was right, Angie thought. Johnny was gone.

"Everyone get away from the door," Boris said.

"No, that door only opens from the inside," Angie said. "They can't use it to get in."

"And at the same time we can't use it to get out," Boris said. "They were waiting for us. It was an ambush. The voice told us what it did knowing we would go this way."

Angie couldn't deny that, nor could she deny that this was her fault for not considering that. The time to blame herself would be later, though, after they got out of here. *If* they got out of here. Angie no longer had much faith in the voice's predictions.

There was a crash from the front of the museum. Broken glass, but not so much that it could have been the whole door. The zombies had probably punched about a fist-sized hole in it. They'd break the rest away any second.

"Keep the lights on," Angie said. "No sense trying to fight them off in the dark. Everyone back into the museum!"

They rushed out of the office, spreading out all over with no obvious plan. They hadn't taken any time to decide what they were going to do if they needed to stand and fight. Jasmine still had her revolver and Angie still had the useless pistol. The museum, lit only by what was spilling out of the office, looked like nothing but a jumbled mess of shadowy artifacts.

Many of which, Angie decided, would work as weapons.

"Grab things to defend yourselves!" Angie said. If anyone planned on asking her what exactly she thought they could use, they didn't get the chance. That was the moment the last of the front door shattered, a zombie flying through the glass as though he'd been thrown. Actually, that was exactly what had happened, Angie saw as a few more stepped through behind him. Several of the zombies had been using the other, who looked like it might have been Archie, as a battering ram. Archie slowly stumbled back to his feet as the others shambled in. Seven of them in total, it looked like, with who knew how many more still outside at the back door.

The light from the office was just enough for Angie to see most of the obstacles as she ran over to the wall and pulled down the murder shovel. The blade wasn't terribly sharp but it would work well enough as a bludgeon. Boris followed suit, grabbing the broken propeller and hefting it, grunting at its surprising weight. Unlike the shovel, the ends of the propeller did look sharp enough to cause some serious damage. Everyone darted around looking for anything at all that might be used to bash or bludgeon, but the two of them had already gotten the best weapons. That, Angie realized, meant they had to be the front line of the attack.

"Do we have a plan?" Boris asked her as all seven zombies shambled around the counter. The massive amount of clutter in this place was just as much a hindrance to them as it was to the living.

"Don't die," she said.

"Maybe something a little more specific?" Boris asked.

Angie responded by calling back over her shoulder to Rudy. "Are there any other exits out of here?"

"If there are, I don't immediately know where," Rudy said. "Bert was the employee here, not me."

"Okay then, I have a plan," Angie said to Boris.

"And that is?"

"We walk out the front door."

She knew if she gave Boris any more time, he would question the sanity of such a plan, so before he opened his mouth she walked forward, moving quickly but carefully around Mukwunaguk's forgotten junk. It was the only plan that had any sort of chance at working. They had a slightly better chance when they vaguely knew what they were up against rather than the back, where every single of person in town could be waiting as a zombie and they wouldn't know.

Of course, that meant she would have to walk straight through seven dead people with a taste for flesh that could burst into flame at any moment. With only a shovel and an empty pistol. It was a good thing she didn't have time to actually think about any of this.

Holding the shovel like a baseball bat, she ran down one of the narrow aisles with a wordless scream straight for the nearest zombie, the one they'd named Jughead. The zombie paused, like she had honestly not expected one of her victims to get this aggressive, if she was capable of expecting anything at this point. Right before Angie swung the shovel, though, she pulled back slightly, suddenly remembering what had happened when Bert shot Becca. The blade of the shovel hit the zombie's outstretched left hand, the side going into the flesh and partially severing her smallest finger. Angie backed up, half-expecting Jughead to burst into flame, but the finger just hung there on a chunk of gristle, not even smoking as it leaked reddish-black fluid. So just general damage to the zombies wasn't enough to send them in napalm mode. Good to know.

She wasn't sure if Boris saw this or if he had just forgotten the possible danger, but he himself didn't hesitate to jab the sharpened propeller end at the next closest zombie. Angie recognized this one as Jodie, one of the volunteer firefighters who would have been at the cabin. Maybe that was where they needed to go to stop this, she thought for a moment. It was apparently where all this had begun, so maybe there was a way to end it there. She thought about that eerie voice on the phone, though, and then the strange footprints burning the pavement. The voice was obviously the one responsible, although Angie still couldn't imagine how, and she had a hunch that the voice and the owner of the footprints were the same person. If that was the case then this mystery woman probably wouldn't be at the cabin anymore. She was somewhere in town, watching over the mayhem she had somehow caused.

Jodie took the propeller blade directly to her chest, stopping her slow shamble just long enough for her to look down at the metal protruding from her breasts and then back at Boris as though to say, "Seriously?" Boris yanked it back out, causing a fountain of sludge that smelled like burnt ashes to spurt from the wound. Jodie only slowed for a moment, though, before stumbling forward again. They all came, slow and shuffling and random, only showing rhythm when they busted out the occasional dance move. It was kind of difficult for Angie to maintain an air of grim determination when they did that.

Angie and Boris backed up. "This isn't going to work unless we can find some kind of weakness," Boris said.

"We can't shoot them in the head, but they can lose body parts without bursting into flame," Angie said. "They can't grab us if they don't have hands, and they can't follow us they can't walk."

Boris nodded. "They can't dance either, so I'd call that a perfect situation."

"Everyone else, we could use some help here!" Angie called back behind her, although she wouldn't look back and take her eyes off the approaching corpses.

"On it!" Kevin called back. "Just buy us some time!"

That was any easy thing for him to say on the other side of the building without a bunch of zombies getting ready to munch on his skull. Archie came up behind Jughead with an amount of speed that Angie didn't think should be possible.

"For the love of God, stop doing that!" Boris screamed at the zombie as he jabbed with the propeller. He just barely missed. "There's supposed to be rules that zombies follow! They're not supposed to be slow one second and fast the next."

Angie didn't bother to argue again about the wisdom of expecting real-world zombies to obey fictional rules, although she herself was getting annoyed that she couldn't be certain what any given zombie might do next. Maybe that was the point. The voice had made it sound like she had designed this particular zombie strain, so why would anyone intentionally trying to cause havoc do it in the way everyone expected?

She swung the shovel again, this time getting more aggressive and aiming at Jughead again. She thwacked the zombie across the face with the flat of the shovel blade. The zombie staggered and then moaned something in protest. It took Angie a second to realize it was suspiciously similar to Vincent Price's first lines in *Thriller*.

"Any time now, guys," Angie called back to the others.

"We've almost got it," Kevin said. "We just need to…oh shit, Kim, watch the glass!"

There was a crash as something broke.

"I'm not sure I want to know what they're doing," Boris said.

Angie heard a strange metallic *sproing* like a breaking spring.

"I meant to do that!" Jasmine called.

Angie changed tactics and took a different grip on the shovel handle, holding it now like a spear and jabbing it directly at Jughead's neck. The metal went deep into her flesh with a sound Angie didn't want to think about. When she pulled the shovel out, Jughead's head fell back like she was a human Pez dispenser, giving Angie way too clear of a view of the viscera inside. Even though the shovel had severed most of the meat in her neck, Angie could still see the spine attached. Jughead kept walking toward her, although with even less coordination than before.

"Coming in for the assist!" Boris yelled, whipping the propeller at Jughead's head like the zombie was a tee-ball. Angie almost told him to stop, worried that the head damage would ignite the zombie. The propeller hit right in soft meat of Jughead's neck, ripping apart the last of flesh and bone to send the head tumbling. The head bounced off the cash register and fell out of sight behind the counter, taking several Gordon Lightfoot CDs with it. Jughead's body continued to fumble around for a second as though it thought it might be able to find and reattach the head before it was too late, then it toppled over to twitch on the ground. After a few seconds, it was still.

Neither the head nor the body burst into flames.

"Nice!" Angie said. "There's your weakness!"

She swung at Jodie, the shovel slicing a gaping hole in her belly which caused some of her intestines to fall out, but Jody didn't seem to notice.

"Okay, here we go!" Kevin yelled. "Angie, Boris, get out of the way! Quick!" Angie didn't think she had the time to turn and see whatever fool thing they were about to try. Instead, she dove over some of the tables, knocking dioramas everywhere. Boris must have done the same because she heard a terrible clattering nearby. No, wait, that wasn't coming from Boris. It was coming from farther back in the museum, back near the...

Tables and display cases flew aside and toppled as the Model-T came barreling down the aisle. Angie only had a quick glimpse of it before she tumbled out of its view, but it looked like the others had haphazardly loaded the tree cross section on the front and, with all of them pushing it from behind, turned it into a battering ram. Glass broke and metal screeched and several zombies made sounds that were suspiciously like surprise. These were followed immediately by multiple squishing noises, like sponges being squeezed and spurting fluid everywhere.

Angie stood up and saw the remains of the Model-T, which had hardly been designed for this kind of thing, in a decidedly bent and broken state next to the front door. It wasn't as broken as several of the zombies, though. Angie could see the limbs of at least one zombie sticking out from between the tree cross-section and the wall. Other zombies were sprawled all over the front, dazed even for walking corpses, many with limbs bent in the wrong directions but only the one that had been smashed was dead. Angie thought she saw the cross-section smoking as something heated it up from the other side.

"This place is about to go up!" she screamed. "Everyone out!"

She recognized that their window of opportunity was short, but Angie refused to be the first one to run out the front door. She needed to make sure that everyone else made it first. This wasn't too hard, considering almost everyone was already there, having helped push their makeshift battering ram. As they went for the door, though, Angie saw one suspicious absence. Megan, up and walking but still unsteady on her feet, was still halfway back down the museum. She hadn't been able to keep up with the others, nor did she look like she understood enough of what was going on to be much help even if she had spontaneously gotten better.

"Megan, come on!" Angie yelled. She seemed to become a little more present at the sound of Angie's voice, at least enough to realize that whatever the hell was going on, it might be a case of life or death.

"Angie?" she asked, looking around at her environment as though this was the first time she'd realized she was in the museum. When she saw the zombies trying to stand up, though, she understood enough to stumble in Angie's direction. Angie ran back to her and grabbed her arm, hoping that Megan would be steady enough to keep her feet as Angie pulled her along. Megan stumbled a couple times but kept up. The rest of the group was out the front door already, and just in time. Archie was back to his feet, and with him Betty and Veronica. Angie thought she had seen some scary librarians in her time, but none that wanted to eat her brains.

Actually, she thought, not a one of the zombies yet had made any indication that they preferred brains over any other tasty body part.

"Braaaaaaaiiiiiins!" Betty and Veronica said in unison.

Well, so much for that.

Angie shoved Megan ahead of her, desperate to get them both out the door before the zombies could grab either of them. They seemed to be in slow mode at the moment, although given their bizarre unpredictability so far, she didn't want to assume they couldn't just speed up at any time. This would have been one of the points where her cohorts might have complained yet again about the zombies not following the rules.

In the end, it wasn't the speed of the zombies that hurt her. It was that she was too distracted by trying to figure out their rules. In a moment of lost concentration while she thought about all of this, Veronica reached out and snagged her with her fingernails. Angie had only enough time to realize that each fingernail, though chipped from the night's activities, was painted white with a Dewey decimal number on each in intricate black. Before she could admire the librarian's dedication, though, she yanked Angie's hand toward her mouth. Her teeth bit down into Angie's flesh and there was a searing hot pain as though she had just stuck her hand in an open flame. Veronica let go with, Angie was almost certain despite the poor quality of the light, a smug smile on her face.

Then she felt a tug at her other hand. Megan. Megan still had a hold of her, and this time she was the one trying to do the saving. Angie followed along, too shocked by the bite to do anything more. This was it. She was dead. She had no idea how long it would take her to turn into a zombie, but judging from what they had all seen so far, it couldn't be more than five minutes. She had a sudden vision of her entire life, so much of it spent in that tiny café, and she wondered if it had all been worth it. Yes, she decided. There might not have been anything spectacular in her life, but it had been well-lived and lived on her terms. If this was all she got, then she decided she could live with it.

However, that didn't mean she was just going to stop and wait for the zombie virus to take her over. She was going to make her last minutes count. She was going to get the rest of these people to safety.

Angie took the lead from Megan again, pulling her out the shattered door and into the swirling snow beyond. It took her several seconds to take stock of the situation, given it all looked like complete chaos. There seemed to be a small group of zombies congregating near the back of the museum and more down either direction on the street. Without being able to stop and count, Angie thought there might be a total of fifty zombies just within visual distance. That was a significant portion of the town's current population. The rest of the people from the museum were running toward the garage, most of them trying to steer well clear of zombies confusedly shuffling around to see that their prey had somehow gotten out without using the back door. Angie saw a set of legs lying on the ground among them, twitching as though in some kind of seizure. Johnny, she realized. That was Johnny turning. At least Angie knew now about how long she had. Not long at all.

It suddenly occurred to her that, knowing she was already dead for all intents and purposes, there was no point in running from the zombies anymore. She gave Megan a shove toward the others, all of whom were following Rudy who had the keys held in his outstretched hand like some magical talisman that would save them. Two of the zombies broke off from the others, finally realizing their targets were on the move. Angie ran right for them, the shovel still in her hand, and wacked the nearest one from behind right in the back of the knee. For something that wasn't supposed to feel pain, the move was surprisingly effective. The zombie might not have felt the damage but Angie had obviously managed to break something vital, because the zombie tumbled and didn't appear like it knew how to get up. The second zombie that had been going for Rudy twisted and lunged at her. Angie made no attempt to avoid it. She even let it get close enough to try biting her shoulder, which wasn't very effective given the thickness of her coat. She gave a wordless scream, partially out of anger that she was about to die and partially because she'd always wanted to do something like that. She jabbed the end of the shovel handle into the zombie's mouth, busting several of its teeth and crushing the soft tissue at the back of the zombie's throat. The zombie pulled away. Angie tried to remove the shovel from its mouth, except the wooden handle was jabbed in there with surprising snugness. The weight of it dragged the zombie's head down until the blade rested on the parking lot pavement, turning the zombie into an unwieldy tripod. Well, at least that meant it couldn't follow anyone. It also meant her weapon was gone, but it wasn't like she was going to need it for much longer.

With nothing but her fists and nails now, Angie placed herself firmly between the advancing zombies and the survivors heading for the garage. She didn't look back at them as Rudy shouted that he had the door open and everyone needed to come in quickly. Angie ignored it. She was a poor excuse for a wall, but she was all they had right now. At the very least, she could slow the zombies down until she turned. If she was lucky, right as she suffered Johnny's unhappy fate, the tour bus would come roaring out of the garage and run her over as she lay twitching on the ground.

Someone grabbed her from behind by the shoulder. "Angie, come on! We've got to get going!" Boris yelled.

"You'll have to go without me," she said. Most of the zombies had paused in their advancement, apparently confused that one of their prey was standing their ground unarmed instead of running. A few weren't so conflicted. Archie, Betty, and Veronica came out the front door, smoke billowing behind them and flickering light indicating that a blaze was starting up in earnest. The three zombies saw her and made a beeline for her. Archie threw in a couple dance moves, but the others didn't follow suit, acting more like the traditional zombies they were supposed to be.

"Are you nuts?" Boris asked. "Get your ass to the bus!" He tried pulling her but she shrugged out of his grip.

"I've been bit!" she said. Boris flinched away as she raised her hand to show the bloody teeth marks. After a couple seconds of blinking at the wound, though, his face became determined.

"Yeah, still not leaving you. Now are you coming or am I going to have to throw you over my shoulder like a caveman asshole?"

Angie took a precious second to look at him. If she stayed behind, she realized, he would try doing it too. He even still had the propeller in hand, ready to use it on the first zombie that came for her. If she stayed behind, he would probably die right along with her.

She looked at her hand again. Angie wasn't sure if she would feel the change coming on or if it would just hit her, but she apparently still had a minute or two. At the very least she could make sure Boris made it to the bus and not sacrifice his sexist ass needlessly.

Angie nodded and ran after Boris as he went through the garage door. Once she was in, he slammed it after them, looking for a lock in the dim light and not finding one.

"It was closed with a padlock," Rudy called from somewhere else in the garage. "You can't lock it from in here."

Boris swore. The door opened inward, at least, and he found some plastic totes full of heavy tools that he slid in front of the door. It might give them a few extra seconds, perhaps a minute at most, but as protection it was decidedly lacking. While Boris messed around with that, the tour bus roared to life behind Angie. The bus, which was one of those smaller, shorter models, was nonetheless still top of the line. Given its place in the local tourism economy, it was one of the few things that the city had made extra effort to pay for. They had not, however, made the same effort with the garage. It was small, only barely large enough for the bus itself to fit in, and it was a tight fit for everyone to pile through the door. If they stayed in here for too much longer, they would likely all suffer from carbon monoxide poisoning. The main door, the one that the bus itself would go out, was still shut against the marauding zombies outside.

Everyone else was inside the bus and Rudy sat behind the wheel, turning the lights on and blinding Angie as she still stood in front of it with Boris.

"Get in!" Boris said.

"I'm about to turn," Angie said. "I can't be in there with the rest of you when it happens. I'll kill you all."

"Jesus, Angie. You are smart and beautiful and you have no idea how much I want to sleep with you—"

"Actually I'm pretty sure I do, and for the last time, I will not—"

"But all the adrenaline in your veins must be making you really dumb."

"...sleep with... Wait. What?"

"Just get in the damn bus and I'll explain it to you when we've all got a moment to breath."

He held out his hand for her to take it. After some hesitation, she did and allowed him to pull her inside the bus. Rudy closed the door behind her.

"Okay everyone," Rudy said. "You just watch this."

"Wait, the main door's still closed," Angie said.

"I know. I've always wanted to do this. Prepare to see something really impressive."

Angie understood what he was about to do and hollered for everyone to get in a seat and hang on tight. With the bus still in park Rudy revved the engine, a mad gleam in his eyes as he looked at the door in front of them. Then he put the bus into drive and slammed his foot on the gas pedal.

The bus rocketed forward a few feet and then slammed into the garage door. Despite their best holds on everything around them, everyone in the bus was thrown out of their seats and hit the floor.

"Shit," Rudy murmured, his eyes dazed from having hit his head on the steering wheel. "That kind of thing usually works in the movies."

"Rudy, I don't think we have much more time for this," Boris said. He pointed out the window at the door they had come through. The zombies had managed to shove it open a few inches and were desperately reaching through.

"Right, right, right." Rudy sighed and put the bus in reverse just enough to get it away from the garage door. "Guess we'll have to do this the boring way. Come on, Bert, where the hell did you put that thing?" He fumbled around in various pockets and compartment near his seat until he pulled out a garage door opener. Angie was afraid that his little stunt might have damaged the door enough that it wouldn't open at all, but when he hit the button the door rose with an agonizing slowness. She could see a couple of zombie legs through the slowly growing gap at the bottom, but most of the zombies were probably congregated over by the smaller door.

When the door was finally high enough that Rudy could drive through, he again put the bus in drive and gunned the engine. The bus hit the few zombies in front of it, most of them disappearing underneath and making an audible squishing sound as the tires rolled over them. One clung to the front of the bus for a couple seconds, long enough for Angie to realize with horror that it was Tina, the dispatcher Rudy had talked to earlier. Her teeth gnashed against the front of the bus as though she thought she could infect the vehicle itself, then she too disappeared underneath. The entire bus shuddered as though it had just hit a speed bump.

Angie remembered why she had been willing to sacrifice herself and stood up. "Rudy, you've got to stop the bus."

"What? The hell I am. I'm not stopping until—"

"You have to let me off. I was bitten."

The entire bus went quiet as the survivors zeroed in on her bloody hand. Kevin and Beth noticeably shied away from her. Megan, interestingly, leaned closer like her only concern was finding a way to stop the bleeding.

"No, Rudy, don't stop. Just keep going," Boris said.

"Boris, seriously," Angie said. "I don't know what kind of misguided chivalry you think you're doing here, but—"

"Angie, just stop for a second and really look at your hand, would you?"

She blinked at him, not understanding, then did as he asked. There was enough blood on her hand now that it was dripping and forming a tiny puddle. She needed to wrap it up soon or else risk losing enough blood to make her woozy. She would also need to clean the wound if she didn't want to get infected, especially since she knew how germy someone's mouth could be.

Which, she realized, was not something she should need to worry about at all anymore. Enough time had passed that she should probably be turning already. Not only that, but her flesh, while torn, hadn't been burned at all. This was the first time since all this had started that she saw one of the zombie bites that hadn't been completely scorched.

Whatever or whoever was causing the zombie outbreak, Angie appeared to be immune from it.

ELEVEN

Angie took off her coat long enough to remove her apron, which she used as a makeshift bandage. There were a lot of questions in her head, and probably a whole lot more in everyone else's, but right now there was only one specific question that had to be answered before anything else.

"Okay," Rudy said. "So just where the hell are we going?"

He was currently driving down James Street, which was the second most important road in town next to Main Street, if any road in town at all could honestly be called important. It also wasn't very long, curving around near its end to merge into the highway. The street appeared to be deserted at the moment. Apparently, any zombies in town had all been converging on the museum. If there were some anywhere else, they didn't see them. Angie would have been tempted to say that they were in the clear, except she highly doubted it would be that easy.

"What about Ontonagon?" Jasmine asked. Angie was sure just saying the word caused her pain. Ontonagon was another town nearby that relied mainly on tourism. The people of Mukwunaguk often thought of it as a poor imitation of their own town, despite Ontonagon being much larger. The rivalry between the two towns was legendary in this tiny corner of the Upper Peninsula.

"Over my dead body," Rudy muttered.

"Given the circumstances, that's entirely a possibility," Kevin said.

"It's the closest town," Boris said. "I don't care about any stupid rivalry. There's no way the zombies have reached it yet. It's our best bet to get help."

"Mmmph," Rudy said. "Maybe it's not going to matter. I don't think we can get that far anyway."

"What do you mean?" Angie asked.

"Take a look at the gas," Rudy said. Angie went up and looked over his shoulder to see the gas needle hovering right over empty.

"What the hell? Why wouldn't they have gassed it up?" Angie

asked.

"They probably didn't think they needed to just yet," Jasmine said. "It's not like anyone was planning on using the bus this soon."

"Can we get gas somewhere?" Angie asked.

Rudy snorted. "The Superior Mart would be closed at this time of night anyway, even if the workers had somehow managed not to be zombies yet. Besides, we're going the wrong way. I'm not sure this is even enough gas for us to turn around at this point, even if we did want to risk going back through the horde."

"And I don't care what anyone says," Beth added. "It's definitely a horde now."

"Do we really have to call them that?" Jasmine asked. "Those were our friends. Family. Lovers."

Angie remembered the zombies they had run over on their way out. Although they had gone under too quickly for Angie to be sure, she thought one of the ones before Tina might have been Brendan Shaw, one of Jasmine's many on-again-off-agains from over the years. She hoped her aunt hadn't seen that.

"So I'm assuming we don't have enough gas to get to Ontonagon?" Angie asked.

"Not even close."

Angie sat back down in her seat and tried to think. Her mind kept wanting to go back to her bleeding hand, to Megan's strange recovery, to all the things the voice had said in the message, but she needed to concentrate on immediate concerns first. She looked out at the darkened road, trying to assess what would be needed for them to survive a little longer. The snow was now swirling furiously outside, forcing Rudy to drive slower than he would have wanted given the situation. Through the storm, though, Angie could still get a decent idea of where they were and which direction they were going. This road would take them closer to Lake Superior, and from there...

She looked at the keys dangling from the bus's ignition. Lots of them. The master back-up set for everything owned and operated by the Mukwunaguk historical society.

"Go to the lighthouse," Angie said.

"I don't like that place," Kim said. "It's haunted."

"Not haunted, mother," Megan murmured. She was rubbing her temples as though she had a headache and still looked completely bewildered by the situation, but the adrenaline of their flight had woken her enough that she would be fine moving around under her own power now. As soon as they all got another quiet moment, they would definitely need to talk to her.

"Why the lighthouse?" Beth asked.

"It's in this direction, and it's just far enough toward the edge of town that people wouldn't normally think to look there. And it's on the other side of the harbor with no trees or anything to hide behind nearby. We'd be able to see zombies walking toward it from a mile away."

"Maybe during the day under clear conditions," Rudy said, gesturing out the front window. "Right now it's neither."

"And it's isolated enough that it will be difficult to get away if they do find us," Kevin said.

"We don't really have much choice but to take that chance," Angie said. "And we need to find somewhere to hole up until the storm is over. It's obvious by now that we might have to walk out of town, and trying to do that at night in a snow storm would be suicide."

"We might be losing the chance to warn everyone on the outside," Beth said. "The zombies could just keep walking without worrying about freezing, especially given their, uh, fiery temperament."

"That's a chance I think we have to take," Angie said. "We have to find somewhere to rest, someplace defensible. If anyone has any better ideas, I'm definitely open to them."

They didn't. Rudy had even already taken the road off the highway that would lead to the lighthouse. It was the only building on this side of the harbor, so they could see it for some distance even through the snow. It was all one building, although parts had been added onto it over the years. That made it an odd conglomeration of white tower, red brick, and yellow siding. There was a chain-link fence around the whole area, another point in its favor in terms of defensibility, and Rudy had to stop the bus long enough for him to get out and unlock the rolling gate. Angie had an idea that they should all get out now and walk the rest of the distance to the lighthouse while Rudy drove the bus somewhere out of sight. It wasn't like they'd be able to use it to make a quick getaway anyway. Rudy grunted his approval, took the key off the ring for the back lighthouse door to give to Angie, then took the rest. He drove the bus away, leaving the rest of them alone here in the middle of nowhere.

Kim's earlier assertion that the lighthouse was haunted was a popular opinion among the townsfolk, and standing out here in the freezing cold staring up at the forlorn tower, Angie could understand the sentiment. Even in the best of times, during the height of tourist season, the lighthouse had the uncanny ability to seem like it was the last building at the edge of the world. It had probably seemed even more so back in the days where it had actually been on the water's edge, before poor civil planning had rendered it useless for its original purpose. It was easy to look out over Lake Superior and feel like there was nothing beyond. The current crash of the waves and howl of the wind didn't help.

"Angie, could we please get the hell inside?" Boris asked. "Not all of us have our coats with us, remember?"

She led them to the back door, which despite its position, was typically the entrance Old Bert had used when starting the tour. Nearby there was a small brick building that housed the lighthouse's circuit breaker and maintenance equipment, but although Angie made note to ask Rudy if one of the keys on the ring would work for it, she still walked past the building for now. They wouldn't want to turn on the power in the lighthouse. It was designed to be a beacon, after all, and they didn't want to alert anyone to their presence here.

Angie unlocked the door and let them all in, counting her charges as they filed past her to a room that wasn't really that much warmer than outside. Kim and Megan, Beth and Kevin, Boris and Jasmine. Including herself and Rudy when he got back, that was eight people. Eight people left from a town of a couple hundred or so. Of course, she had no way of being certain that they were the only survivors, but the odds for everyone else didn't look good.

However, she was also aware that this number was higher than it was supposed to be. Once they were all in and settled, this needed to be the first thing they discussed.

This first room had originally been intended as a kitchen and pantry, the last room that had been added to the house back when people were actually supposed to live in it. It was pitch black in there as the room didn't have any windows, but that was just fine for now. Once they spread out, they would need to find ways to cover up the windows anyway. After some cursing and fumbling, Beth managed to get the batteries back in their two flashlights (since one had been lost in their hustle to get out of the museum) and they were able to walk around a little without banging their shins into more artifacts of a bygone time. While technically as much a museum as the place they had just left, the lighthouse had been laid out to look as much as possible like it once had when it was inhabited. The shelves in here had old cans and jars on the shelves, a small table, an old fashioned cast iron stove, and a primitive laundry wringer. None of this stuff was actually useful anymore, unfortunately. Several of them eyed the stove with heavy sighs as they shivered.

"Okay, so now what, fearless leader?" Boris asked her. Despite the sarcasm of the question, he sounded sincere enough, and judging from the looks on everyone else's faces, they felt the same way. She was indeed their leader, and their survival or death relied entirely on her.

Angie thought about it and then handed out some tasks. They were going to have to stay here until the storm was over and they could try walking out of town, preferably in the day when it wasn't as cold. So, although they hopefully wouldn't be here too long, they still needed to make this place livable. There were a few small windows on this floor, all of them high up on the walls because the base of the lighthouse was partially built into a small hill. She assigned Boris and Jasmine to find anything they could use to cover the windows up so they could use the flashlights with risk of being seen. Kevin searched in a closet and found a small gas-powered space heater used for the rare occasions when someone needed to be in the lighthouse during the off season. Angie, Beth, and Kevin went up to the second and third floors looking for any extra pillows, blankets, or anything else they could use to rest and warm up. These were the floors that had actual beds and amenities, many of them almost as old as the lighthouse itself, and they were kept looking ready to use in order to give tourists the proper idea of old-style lighthouse life.

The bottom floor of the lighthouse, the one they had come in on, was technically more of a basement. After the kitchen was a dining room that had been converted into a more museum-like space, with various utensils, china, and other ephemera of daily life from the early 1900s kept in glass cases. Beyond there was a small room with rickety stairs that led up to the real first floor. Here there was a study, a living room and one of the bedrooms. Again, this floor was dressed to look like someone still lived in it with a few out of place items for the tourists to view, most noticeably the old foghorn in the living room. Old Bert had always taken what Angie thought was a perverse pleasure in telling the tourists to cover their ears and then crank its handle, shaking the entire lighthouse with its piercing bass rumble. In front was the main door, although it was never used, and a narrow metal stairwell that spiraled upward. The second floor was all bedrooms, all of them small with low ceilings thanks to the sloping roof. Taking the stairs past this floor brought tourists to the top of the lighthouse tower where they would have to go outside onto a rickety platform that surrounded the light itself. The light room could only be accessed through a small hatch that tourist had to get down and crawl through, and only four or five of them could fit in it at a time provided they scrunched together. Angie suspected they were going to have to send someone up there later to act as a lookout, but for now they left the tower alone.

By the time they had all assembled back in the dining room, Rudy had returned. He'd remembered what happened back at the museum and stopped in the maintenance shed before coming in, so they now had more weapons- shovels, hoes, a very large pair of hedge trimmers, and various other gardening implements. There was enough that everyone had a weapon now, even if most of them were of dubious use in a fight. Rudy also told Angie to hold out her hand and gave her a full magazine for Old Bert's gun.

"He had it stashed under the seat in the bus," Rudy explained. "I found it when I was searching for a first aid kit." He indicated her bitten hand, which had stopped bleeding for now but throbbed horribly. Angie kept expecting it to finally grow dark with charred skin, the sign that she was finally turning. All it did instead was make her desperately wish for some pain killers.

"Did you find one?" Angie asked.

"Not in the bus, but I'm sure there's got to be one in here somewhere. This decrepit old place is full of ways for fool tourists to injure themselves."

Angie nodded. They hadn't found one so far but that didn't mean it wasn't here. At the moment, though, she was more interested in the magazine.

"Why the hell did he have this in the bus?" Angie asked.

"Knowing Old Bert, he probably expected one of the tourists to rob him or something. That, or he *really* didn't want anyone taking a selfie with him."

Angie decided not to question it and instead silently thanked the crotchety old man, wherever he might be now.

"We should all get some rest," Angie said, turning to the others. Every single one of them was staring at her, hanging on her every word. Kevin, however, seemed decidedly unnerved.

"Can't we talk about something first?" he asked.

"What?" Angie asked.

"The fact that several of us are supposed to be dead. And aren't."

Angie thought at first of her own bite wound, then remembered with a start that, according to the voice on the message, Kevin wasn't supposed to be here. He was supposed to be shambling around in the zombie horde right next to Johnny.

"Well, I'm not sure yet about me," Angie said, raising her wounded hand for all to see, "but I've got a general idea why you didn't die."

"Please enlighten us," Jasmine said. "Because I'm sure we can use any news at all that might make us less freaked out."

"It's exactly what I was saying earlier," Angie said. "Something went wrong early in the voice's plan."

"We've got to stop just calling it 'the voice' or 'the message.' We need to give her some kind of name to identify her."

"Sabrina," Kevin said.

"Huh? Why Sabrina?" Boris asked.

"Well duh. We've already had Archie, Betty, Veronica, and Jughead. What else are you going to call the apparently magical female that hangs around them?"

"We're not calling her Sabrina," Boris said.

"I think that name's pretty," Kim said.

Angie waved her uninjured hand to stop the argument before it could really start. "Fine. Whatever. She's Sabrina until we have something else to call her. Her name's not what's important. What's important is the butterfly effect we're causing. Going into the museum there were two people there that weren't supposed to be. Megan and Beth."

"Uh, I'm still not one hundred percent sure what's going on here," Megan said. Her voice still had a slight slur to it but she was standing steady without any help now, and she had managed to be some help while searching for supplies.

"We'll get to all that in a second, I think," Angie said. "So we had those two with us when we weren't supposed to. And that changed things." She thought about it for a second. "Two things, as far as I can see so far.

"One, Kevin," she said, holding up a finger. "Somehow the fact that Beth was still alive saved him. Although I'm not entirely sure how."

"I think maybe I was supposed to get dragged out the back door with Johnny," Kevin said. "That seems like the most likely place and time."

"Then why didn't you?" Boris asked. "What little thing out of place kept you from being at that door?"

Even in the dim light, Angie thought she could see him blush. "Uh, I guess I was, uh, a bit tired."

"Tired?" Boris asked.

Angie figured it out immediately and had to fight not to smile. "You don't need to say, Kevin."

"No, I want to know," Boris said.

"Uh, I was slower because, uh…"

"It was me," Beth said. "I'm the one who tired him out."

Boris still didn't seem to get it for a few seconds. "What are you even…?"

Beth twitched her eyebrows in a suggestive manner and rubbed a finger over her bottom lip as though she were wiping something away.

"Oh," Boris said. "Uh, I see."

"Wait, I don't watch too many horror movies," Jasmine said, "but isn't that kind of thing against the rules? You know, sex is supposed to kill you, not save you?"

"Good thing this is real life, then," Beth said.

"Yeah, sure, if an invasion of dancing zombies who don't always conform to zombie rules could ever be real," Boris said.

"The point being that Beth's presence changed the way things were supposed to be." Angie paused, not sure whether she wanted to bring this up, but it was something they would have to discuss eventually. "And Megan's presence was the reason I got bit."

"Yeah, it's time to talk about that," Rudy said, a hint of distrust creeping into his voice.

"Wait, back up first," Megan said cautiously. "My memory of the last couple of hours is pretty fuzzy. Could someone fill me in on what the hell has been going on?"

"Actually, we were hoping you could tell us," Angie said. Nonetheless, she gave an abbreviated version of everything that had happened from the moment Megan's car had crashed in front of the Gitchigumi Café. Despite her better condition now, Megan paled as she seemed to realize how much of a role she'd played in it all.

"So what did you mean about me being the reason you were bit?" Megan asked. The guilt in her voice was tangible and made Angie feel bad for her.

"Well, I didn't say it was your fault. But I stayed back to help you get out and that's when I got bit. Judging from Sabrina's prediction, that wasn't supposed to happen. I was supposed to survive."

"But you did survive," Boris pointed out.

"And do we have any idea how?" Jasmine asked.

"I don't have a clue," Angie said. "Which brings us back to you, Megan. You were the first one who was supposed to succumb to the zombie virus, or whatever it is. And you didn't. So the question is why?"

Megan stared at the wall for several seconds. Judging by the look on her face, whatever she was thinking or remembering wasn't pleasant. "I don't know."

"Were you out by that cabin?" Angie asked. "Is that where you were bitten?"

Again, Megan hesitated for a long time before she answered. "I wasn't bitten by a zombie. Or I don't think it was a zombie. It was…something else."

It was obvious that thinking about what had happened to her was traumatic, but Angie couldn't help but feel a faint glimmer of happiness that they might finally be about to get answers. "What was it, Megan?"

"I think it was, uh, based on what you guys said was on my phone, I guess it was Sabrina."

"So you saw her?" Boris asked.

Before Megan could answer, Kim grabbed her by the shoulders and pulled her away from the rest of the group. "You all stop this right now. You're upsetting her."

Megan tried to shrug Kim's hands off her, but the woman's fingernails were hooked into her daughter's clothes like talons. "Mom, stop. Please. I can take care of myself."

"No, you can't. You need me, you always have."

"We need to know what happened or what you saw," Angie said gently. "It's important. It could tell us what's really happening. It might even give us some idea of how to stop it."

Kim tried to pull Megan farther away from the group. Megan finally managed to twist out of her grip, then walked right up to Angie. The way she got so close yet looked away from Angie's eyes at the last second made Angie's breath catch in her throat. She knew that look. She'd seen it in others, although some had hid it better than others. Boris looked at her in a similar way, although without the demure bashfulness. Although she supposed she could be wrong, Angie thought Megan might have a crush on her. How long had that been there, she wondered? And more importantly, what did she feel about it?

"I was on the shore," Megan said, still not meeting anyone's eyes. "Yeah, it was near the cabin those tourists were renting."

"What were you doing out there?" Kim asked, her voice sounding bizarrely harsh for such a simple question. Megan tensed, the movement of a child afraid someone was about to beat them. Angie thought to the bottle of pills in Megan's pocket, wondering if the two things were somehow related. After all, Megan didn't strike her as the kind that had that many secrets.

Or maybe not. She thought again to the way Megan had looked away. Perhaps she *was* the kind to keep herself hidden.

"It doesn't matter," Angie said. "Go on."

"There was...uh, an explosion."

The words came tumbling out of Megan's mouth so fast Angie thought she might be afraid of them, like if they were with her for too long they might do something terrible. Her narrative wasn't always the clearest, but no one dared interrupt her. On any other day, the story Megan told would have been completely unbelievable, yet they had already seen so much tonight that they story of a burned woman who wouldn't die didn't seem so far-fetched.

"I don't really remember much after she bit me," Megan said. "Just bits and pieces. I think I remember her talking into my phone. She said a few other things too. Then she pushed me off, and then it's just fragments of the things you guys already told me."

"What else did she say?" Boris asked.

"I don't know," Megan responded.

"Think, Megan. Please," Angie said. She resisted the urge to reach out and grab her shoulders. "Anything at all that you remember might be the key to getting us all out of this."

"I said I don't know!" Megan yelled, backing away from everyone. Yet she looked Angie in the eye finally, and the blind, uncomprehending fear Angie saw there told her that Megan did, in fact, remember something. Something she didn't want to say.

Angie looked around at everyone else. "Megan, would you maybe want to talk about this with me alone?"

"No, you can't do that," Kim said. "She's fragile. She needs to rest."

"Please stop," Megan said, although her voice was low, cowed, like she'd been in this situation with her mother before and knew exactly how it would end. The look in her eyes didn't match her tone, however. There was fire there, anger.

"Kim, it's okay," Angie said, making it very clear with her tone that she was going to take Megan aside whether Kim liked it or not. Kim might not have the best grasp of subtleties, but she could tell when Angie wasn't going to put up with any of her shit. Kim silently backed away, and while everyone else stared Angie led Megan up the stairs to the first floor where they would have a small measure of privacy.

Angie would have preferred they sit on a couch or something, but the only couch in the living room was an antique that probably wouldn't have supported even the two of them at once. Instead, Angie led her to the bedroom where they sat on the bed. There were still some windows on this floor that they hadn't covered, so neither of them dared use a flashlight, instead having to rely on the tiny amount of ambient light filtering in through the snow-covered windows. Angie had been in here before, though, and she knew the basic layout. The bedroom was fairly plain, much as it had been when it was actually in use, with the only noticeable decoration being a framed black and white photograph of Samuel Haecker, one of the several men who had once been the lighthouse keeper. He was the most notorious and legendary because he only had one hand, the result of a drunken attempt to stop a firing cannonball that was being shot off at a Fourth of July celebration. Local legend persisted that he had wandered back to the lighthouse and fallen asleep in this very bed for a short time before going to a doctor, and that his blood could still be found on this bed if one only knew where to look. Angie had never wanted to look.

Megan sat on the bed first, her head lowered, while Angie sat next to her being sure to keep a respectful distance. "Megan, what is it you're not telling anyone?"

"I don't want to say it," she murmured.

"Megan, please. It might be important."

Megan didn't answer for a long time. Angie resisted the urge to ask more questions. They needed any information Megan had sooner rather than later, and there was no telling how much every little second counted. At the same time, though, Angie got the impression that pushing her would only get Megan to clam up permanently.

Finally, Megan murmured something under her breath. Angie

politely asked her to speak up.

"I said have you ever wished that you just weren't here anymore?"

Angie's brow furrowed in puzzlement. It was an odd question to which Megan should have already known the answer. Everyone wanted to leave Mukwunaguk at some point. Even the lifers would occasionally talk about finding better prospects somewhere else.

Then Angie realized that "here" didn't mean Mukwunaguk. Megan meant the world in general. Angie immediately believed she knew what Megan was going to say, and she desperately wanted to reach out and hug the girl, to tell her that everything would be okay. Given the current situation, though, that would obviously be a lie.

"Yes," Angie answered truthfully. "I've been there."

"I was there to kill myself," Megan said. The words came out breathlessly, as though she had just been running a marathon and this was her final sprint as she crossed the finish line. She sat up a little straighter, looking as though she had just physically removed something from herself that had been pulling her down. "Or maybe I really wasn't. I suppose I was there to *not* kill myself. Does that make any sense?"

Angie nodded. She wasn't completely sure that she did get it. She knew, though, that the only thing that mattered was that the words were meaningful to Megan. They were something she could cling to, something she could use to pull herself back up.

"I had meds," Megan continued. "I was either going to take them or drown myself. I took them. But..." Now she hesitated again, her brief show of confidence vanishing. "That woman said something to me after I was bit. She said she was glad I had chosen to die, because she could use me. She said I would have purpose in death that I never had in life."

Megan stopped. Angie didn't interject anything. This wasn't exactly the kind of conundrum she'd ever prepared herself to face, trying to tell someone suicidal that the weird burning zombie woman didn't really mean she was useless.

"I've been thinking," Megan said. "Maybe that's what made the difference. She was acting like I had chosen to die. But I'd chosen to live. I'd chosen to fight. Maybe that's why I didn't become the zombie I was supposed to. Because I'd simply made up my mind not to be."

Megan looked at Angie as though for approval of her theory. Angie shrugged and said nothing. In truth, it kind of sounded like hooey to her, but who was to say it wasn't correct? There were a lot of things about this night that had defied basic logic. Angie supposed that if Megan wasn't right, that she hadn't just survived by sheer force of will, then the actual answer might as well have been just as, if not more, ridiculous.

"That's what I didn't want to say in front of everybody else," Megan said. "But there's one more thing, something that woman said that I didn't really understand. I just think maybe it's important."

"What was it?"

"I'm not sure I can remember it all. It's kind of garbled in my head. I was pretty out of it by that point, remember. It was…it was strange, I guess. Like in the movies where a villain monologues about their plans even though it makes no sense to stop right there and do so. As though the only reason the villain is doing it is that they actually know the audience is there and needs to understand what's going on. I think… I might not be remembering this right, but I think she even turned around and acted like she was speaking to a bunch of people."

"And what did she say?" Angie asked.

"I think she said she was doing this for them. She might have called them the Legion. Or maybe the masses. Massive legion. Whatever. She said that if what she did here pleased them then she would only be the first. Her siblings would come."

Now Angie was really starting to get confused. "I don't think I understand."

"She said that if they were pleased, there would be three more stories. That part I remember very clearly. She called what she was doing a story. She said she knew that what she was doing was risky, addressing them directly, but she thought the result would be worth it."

"Are you sure that's what she said?" Angie asked. "Because that doesn't make a lot of sense."

"I know it doesn't, and no, I'm not sure. Like I said, I was pretty groggy. But I know what she said next. This I remember clearly. She said the names of her three siblings."

Megan stopped. It was obvious she didn't want to continue.

"And?" Angie gently prodded. "What were the names?"

Megan looked her directly in the eye. "War, Famine, and Death."

TWELVE

"Pestilence?" Boris asked. "You're seriously saying that the woman responsible for this is one of the Four fucking Horsemen of the Apocalypse?"

"I don't know what I'm saying," Angie said. She'd left Megan upstairs to sleep on the bed while she came down to talk strategy with the others. She'd wanted to talk to Megan some more, and it seemed obvious to her that Megan wanted to say a few things herself that were on a more personal level. Angie had to admit that she was open to the idea of more between the two of them, but all thoughts of that would have to wait until later. For now, Megan was still not at one hundred percent and she needed her rest, especially if shit was going to hit the fan before the sun rose. And judging from what Sabrina, or rather Pestilence if that was who she really was, had said on the message, there would be at least one more major confrontation. The woman's predictions hadn't been one hundred percent accurate, but they were close enough that Angie knew they needed to prepare.

Angie had relayed most of Megan's information to the others, leaving out the more personal issues Megan had been dealing with. They stood around her now, their eyes wide and looking frantic in the dim glow of their flashlights. Angie certainly couldn't blame any of them for their disbelief. She herself was having a hard time with this. Somehow, pop culture had prepared her for the possibility of a zombie apocalypse, but not at the behest of one of the Four Horseman. And that wasn't even the end of the weird details, if the theory developing in Angie's mind was correct.

"So is this it?" Jasmine asked. "Is this really the end of the world?"

"Not exactly how I expected it," Rudy said.

"I know," Kevin said. "It's like, 'Come on, make up your mind. Pick a set of zombie rules and stick with it. Pick a post-apocalyptic theme and don't stray.'"

"Kevin, honey, this is the real world," Beth said. "Things are usually not as simple as all that."

"Actually, based on what Megan said, I would almost think he's on to something," Boris said. "The zombies are slow sometimes and fast others. Sometimes they shamble, sometimes they dance. They infect others by a bite, like a plague, but they're obviously magical in nature. And the fact that they only burst into flame when shot in the head, the only way we typically think to kill a zombie, it's almost like…"

He waved his hand, unable to think of the right term. Angie had it for him.

"It's like we're being trolled," she said. "Like everything about this situation has been specifically designed to screw with us. And if Megan is remembering any of Pestilence's monologue correctly at all, then I think that's exactly what's happening."

"So this Pestilence, uh, is that really what we're going to call her from now on?" Rudy asked. Everyone else shrugged. "This Pestilence is working for someone else. Who?"

"Megan said something about masses or a legion. So demons?" Boris asked. "That would keep with the Biblical aspects here."

"Except even the Biblical aspects are all messed up," Kevin said. "I spent my whole childhood in Sunday school, so I should know by now that this doesn't look anything at all like what the Book of Revelation describes."

"Whatever force is getting Pestilence to do this, he or she or it or them has to be powerful," Angie said. "But it's like they don't have any direct influence over what's going on. They can only observe. Almost like Pestilence is putting on a show for them."

"So you're saying they could be watching us right now as we have this conversation?" Jasmine asked.

"Could be," Angie said.

They all stirred nervously. Angie felt the most bizarre urge to turn to the nearest wall, where a camera might have been if this were a movie, and wave cheekily to whatever obscene force might be observing her. But she wasn't sure she was ready to accept this theory yet. Even with everything else that had been happening, that was just a step too far for her mind to take.

"So what are we going to do about it?" Boris asked.

"If this really is one of the Four Horsemen, and Pestilence

really is doing this to please some other force, then there's a very simple answer," Angie said.

"And that would be?" Beth asked.

"Make sure this other force isn't pleased."

"Oh, is that all?" Kevin asked. "Displease some unknowable group of entities that are paying attention to our exploits right now. Doesn't sound like that plan could go wrong at all."

"Hell, it's not even really a plan," Beth said.

Kim made a *hmpf* noise. "And people say I'm the one that has weird delusions."

"Look, it already seems to be happening," Angie said. "It's been happening all night. Pestilence thought she had everything planned out, but we're not playing by her rules."

"But how do we know we're not?" Jasmine asked. "For all we know, us thinking we have some kind of advantage was exactly what she wanted. Whoever she's trying to please, maybe they enjoy watching us think we can live when some twist later means that we all die. Isn't that usually how it works in horror movies? The heroes think they won and then, bam, bloodbath?"

"Jasmine, Angie, you know I love you both," Rudy said. "You're the closest thing to family I have. But even in the current situation, your talk is starting to sound crazy. This isn't a horror movie. We're not going to find some secret way to defeat the villain that comes completely out of left field and doesn't actually make sense to anyone who thinks about it for too long."

Angie scratched her head and sheepishly looked away. "Um, actually…"

Rudy sighed. "Of course. That's what I get for that."

Boris laughed. "Why do I get the feeling this is going to be really rich?"

"I was thinking about some things Megan said. Um, things I'm not actually supposed to talk about with you guys." Angie paused, wondering if there was any way she could get around this without discussing Megan's suicidal plans. If she didn't want the others to know then she had that right, but one particular detail had stuck out to her, one that had got her mind racing and making connections. Exactly like Rudy had said, it was absolutely ridiculous. Made no sense whatsoever. Yet the seeds had been planted in their story from the very beginning, and she would be stupid to ignore this one, vital coincidence.

"I didn't turn," Angie said, holding up her roughly bandaged hand. "Neither did Megan. Johnny did. Everyone else we've seen so far did. If I'm right there might even be a few more survivors out there, if they didn't just get ripped apart or burned to a crisp."

"Well, are you going to tell us or are you just pausing to make the moment more dramatic?" Kevin asked.

"Just give me a second, will you? So there's obviously something Megan and I must have in common, yet different enough that she still looked for a while like she was going to turn while I didn't at all. And there's only one answer that I can think of. Right before Pestilence attacked her, Megan took some of these."

Angie pulled out the pill bottle from where she had been keeping it in her pocket for – yes, she had to own up to it – dramatic effect. She'd slipped it away from Megan right as she was falling asleep. Angie knew Megan wouldn't want anyone here knowing that she'd taken medication, especially not her mother, but there was no avoiding telling at least this much.

Kim audibly gasped, even sounded like she wanted to cry, as though the thought of her daughter on prescription drugs was the worst possible fate. Everyone else, however, looked at the bottle with utter confusion.

"What even is that?" Kevin asked.

"A pill bottle, dummy," Beth said. "The orange color didn't give it away?"

"Well duh, but what's in it?"

"It's a depression medication," Angie said. "A very specific kind. And I take exactly the same one."

"You're serious?" Boris asked. "You think this is what kept you from turning into a zombie?"

"Megan took one for the first time right before she was attacked. It was in her but hadn't had a chance to get through her whole system yet. Whereas I take it on a regular basis. That's why I wasn't affected at all."

"Um, that's very, uh…" Jasmine started. Boris finished the thought for her.

"Stupid. The word you're looking for is stupid."

"Uh, yeah," Kevin said. "As far as weaknesses for evil zombies and ways to stop the apocalypse, that's pretty lame."

"Sounds to me like this is all just a plot by Big Pharma to poison us all," Kim said. Despite the bizarre amount of hysteria and fear in her voice, everyone pretty much ignored her.

"Yes, it is kind of lame," Angie said to Kevin. "And maybe that's exactly why it's going to work. For better or worse, it's going to be what keeps us all from getting infected. And I bet that whatever or whoever is watching us is going to think it's dumb as well. Like a cheat or a copout. And they'll take it out on Pestilence. Any plans Pestilence has to get this all to spread will be stopped in its tracks."

"You're making an awful lot of assumptions," Rudy said. "Most of this is just speculation. We have no idea if anything you're saying would actually work."

"No, we don't," Angie said. "But what else are we going to do? Here's one thing I think we can all agree on: Pestilence isn't done with us tonight. She said as much in her message. Even if she doesn't have everything as well planned as she thinks she does, she seemed pretty convinced that at least one more thing was going to happen. So here's our options: we can wait for dawn and do our best to fight off the horde if or when it comes. Or we can do the exact same thing but also each of you take a pill. Maybe it will work and maybe it won't, but even if it doesn't you have absolutely nothing to lose by giving it a shot."

Boris glared at the bottle in her hand. "Any side effects?"

"It might make you a tad on the drowsy side. I suppose it's possible one of you might have a horrible side effect, but I doubt you'll feel anything with just one pill."

"Will one pill even do anything?" Kevin asked.

Angie shrugged. "It seems to have worked for Megan."

"If that's really what saved her," Beth said.

Angie shrugged again. It was very possible that she was missing something vital and the pills had nothing to do with their immunity. But if she was wrong, they would be no worse off than they already were. If she was right, she might just be saving a few lives here.

"So what, we all take one and whammo, we're safe?" Kevin asked as Angie opened the childproof cap and dumped a number of the pills into her hand.

"You're safe from being turned, theoretically," Angie said. "Megan took one immediately before she was bitten and she looked for a while like she was going to turn, but didn't. I've been on them for a long time and nothing happened to me at all. I guess that, if this works, the rest of you would be somewhere in between." She picked one pill up and held it out, waiting for the first person to take it from her.

"Does anyone else think this is supposed to be a metaphor or something?" Boris asked. "Like someone or something wants a deeper meaning behind this moment?"

"If it is, it's a dumb, obvious metaphor," Beth said. She took the pill from Angie and immediately swallowed it, no preamble. "Blech. Chalky."

"Usually you're supposed to drink something with them," Angie said. "But yeah. I've had to deal with that taste for years now."

Kevin followed suit, and then Jasmine, Boris, and finally Rudy. Kim was the only one who didn't take one. She had backed herself into a corner as though the pills would sprout legs and come after her, shaking her head emphatically every time someone swallowed one.

"You're just playing into their hands," Kim muttered. "Big Pharma has you now. They'll never let go. They'll squeeze you and squeeze and—"

"Jesus Christ, shut the hell up," Boris said. "I think I like it a lot better when you just stand around acting creepy." He said this last word with no self-awareness or irony. Despite their situation, Angie had to suppress a small laugh.

"So what, now we're good?" Kevin asked.

"Now you can't turn into a zombie," Angie said. "Hopefully. I could still be wrong, so I would suggest avoiding getting bit. But I wouldn't call that safe. There's still that whole thing where zombies like to rip your head apart and eat your brains."

"Oh," Kevin said. "Yeah, I guess there is that."

"You're all zombies already," Kim hissed under her breath.

"That what Big Pharma wants, you know. You're now their willing slaves and—"

Jasmine wordlessly hit Kim upside the back of the head. She finally shut up.

THIRTEEN

They took shifts of three people each. One each would guard the kitchen door, the front door, and sit in the light room at the top of the tower. The person in the tower had the most important job, watching to see if anything was coming for them out of the snowstorm that seemed to be slowly winding down. They only stayed up there for half an hour at a time, which was still way to long for those that hadn't managed to take their coats with them when leaving the café, switching out with one of the others. They'd do this in spans of about two hours at a time while the others tried to sleep. After some arguing and finagling, it was decided that the shifts would consist of Kevin, Beth, and Rudy on one while Jasmine and Boris joined Angie on the other. Angie had tried to change this grouping, but for once the others asserted themselves and overruled her. Kevin and Beth wanted to be able to spend their rest time together, which Angie thought was a good way for neither of them to get any rest at all. She was at least grateful that she'd gotten Rudy to join their shift, as she expected he wouldn't let them get away with slipping off with each other while they were supposed to be on guard duty.

The other thing Angie objected to with this arrangement was that it put her on the same shift as Boris. This wasn't so bad during the first two hours when they were actually on the lookout, but as she had been afraid of, he came to her once their shift was over and it was time for them to sleep. Megan was still asleep in the bed on the first floor with her mother sleeping on the floor next to her. Everyone had agreed that Megan would need more rest than everyone else if she was going to be functional when it finally came time for action, and without even having to discuss it they'd all come to the consensus that Kim was too unreliable to help them. While those two were on the first floor, the rest huddled in the dining room downstairs, since Angie thought it would be better if they were all close together in the event something went wrong. It would be much more comfortable sleeping on the beds on the second floor, but if the zombies found them it would take too much precious time running all around the lighthouse trying to find and warn everyone.

This was where Boris found her after their shift. Jasmine, who out of the three of them had been the last one in the tower, immediately came down after being relieved, made a nest out of every blanket, sheet, and piece of clothing she could find, and huddled under it to shiver herself to sleep. Angie sat in the corner smoking and using one of the china tea cups from the glass cases as an ashtray. She'd been jonesing for a cigarette for over an hour now, but going outside at all was a risk. She hadn't even wanted to light up in the tower for fear that the red ember of her cigarette would get caught by the mirrors and provide a faint beacon for the zombies to see. The inside of the lighthouse was supposed to be a strict no smoking zone, but she figured there probably wasn't anyone left in Mukwunaguk who would bother enforcing such a law at the moment.

She'd hoped that Boris would just come in from the front door and go to sleep, but he instead hunkered down not five feet from her. Something on her face must have warned him that she wasn't in the mood, because he moved a little bit farther away before he spoke.

"Can we talk for a bit?" he asked.

"I suppose. Although I reserve the right to stop listening."

"I think maybe you have the wrong idea about me."

Angie raised an eyebrow. "This ought to be interesting."

"You seem to be under the impression that I'm some kind of creeper. I'm not."

"So those weren't pick-up artist techniques you were trying to use on me at the café after all?"

"Look, I'm sorry if I offended you. I just have never tried to get the attention of someone like you before."

"Someone like me?"

"Well, you know."

"No, I don't know. Explain it to me. But if I were you, I would keep in mind that I'm currently holding a lit cigarette."

"Uh..." He stared at the cigarette, and although it was hard to tell in the minimal light it looked like he scooted a few more inches away. "You know, uh, someone who's, er, bisexual."

She cocked her head, pretty sure where this was going, but not wanting to believe he was actually going to dig himself into this particular hole. "And what exactly would the difference be between catching the interest of a bisexual woman and that of a hetero woman?"

Boris looked thoroughly confused. "They're not the same."

"How are they not the same?"

"Well, you know, you're more interested in sex than a straight woman."

Angie looked at her cigarette and imagined putting it out on his arm. She would never actually do that, but the temptation was there. "You're saying that because I'm bisexual you think I'm easy."

"Uh, no, that's not the words I would use…"

"You think I'm bi because I don't care who I get it from?"

"Well…"

"And what, if I had sex with you, I'd see the light and make up my mind and never have sex with anyone else ever again."

"Hey now, don't go putting words into my mouth."

"I'm bisexual because sometimes I'm attracted to women and sometimes I'm attracted to men. I'm not confused. It would not mean that I've 'made up my mind' if I settle down with one gender or the other. And my sex drive is no more or less than anyone else's. Being bi doesn't mean I don't have standards. That's why you're interested in me, isn't it? Because you think I don't have standards?"

"That's harsh. You don't need to be mean about it."

"I'm not interested in you and you weren't interested in me until I came out. Then you started acting borderline disturbing. I know you think you're a nice guy and I should see that, but you're being possessive and entitled. The first time I subtly said no should have been enough."

He was quiet for a long time. When he spoke again, she expected him to have some witty retort, or maybe to call her a bitch or do one of the myriad other things that guys like him would resort to when a woman asserted herself as something other than a man's property. To her surprise, though, he only said two words.

"I'm sorry."

"I, uh, what?"

"I said I'm sorry. Maybe you're being a little harsh on me, but then again maybe you're right. Most of that isn't the kind of thing I usually think of."

She looked away from him. "Well, I have to think about it all the time. You're not the only one who's wanted into my pants without considering whether or not I wanted them there." She took one last drag on her cigarette before stubbing it out in the teacup and then looking back at him. "Although I do have to admit you're the first one to admit they were a douchebag."

"Hey, the word *douchebag* never actually came out of my mouth."

"Well, it was close enough."

"So what do you say, want to have sex?"

She flicked her cigarette butt at him, which he dodged easily. "That better have been a joke, or else you're not leaving this lighthouse alive."

"It was," he said with a smile, although it disappeared almost immediately. "Do you really think we are?"

"We are what?"

"We're going to get out of here alive."

She shrugged. "I don't know."

"Other than when you were bit, you've been handling this disturbingly well, you know that?"

"I guess it hasn't really set in yet. I'm still in crisis mode. I'm sure once we escape for good, I'll be a gibbering mess."

"Kind of hard to believe, given what we've seen of you so far," Boris said. "I have to admit, I wouldn't have thought I'd ever be relying on a waitress as my leader during the zombie apocalypse."

"I don't think it's the apocalypse. Not yet, at least. Not if we can get out and warn the rest of the world."

"Yeah, well, the point remains."

"Watch it. You're getting dangerously close to being insulting again."

"What I mean is, you're not military. You're not a cop. You don't have any kind of specialized training for any of this. Hell, you're not even a nurse that can patch us up. So why is it that so few of us in this group have died so far?"

"I don't know," Angie said with a shrug. "A will to live? Seen too many zombie stories on TV? Or maybe it's just entirely possible that an average woman in a small town can be, oh I don't know, capable?"

"Hm. Point taken." Boris was quiet for several seconds. "Okay, I know I'm really at risk of sounding like a total pig here, but are you sure you don't want to have sex? Because really, you can't tell me that if we are going to die you don't want to get some before you go."

"You really don't know when to quit do you?" Angie said. "Yes, it would be nice to have sex before I die but no, never in a million years would it be with you."

"Just thought I'd check one last time. Out of curiosity, though, if your life did in fact depend on having sex with someone in the lighthouse right now, who would it be?"

Angie's mind flashed uncontrollably to Megan, although she didn't let herself dwell on the young woman for too long. "Quit being gross already."

"I'll have sex with you," a groggy voice said from one of the corners. Both Angie and Boris looked to see Jasmine's head slowly coming out of her cocoon of blankets.

"Please tell me you're not talking to me, Aunt Jasmine," Angie said.

"Don't be ridiculous." Jasmine turned to blink at Boris. "So what do you say?"

"Uh, no offense, Jasmine, but you're like twice my age."

"So? Who cares? If we both die, it's not like it will matter."

"No one else is going to die," Angie protested.

"Come on, Boris. You're a young guy desperate to get his rocks off. I'm a more mature woman that knows what she's doing and would like an orgasm or two before I die."

Angie looked back at Boris and was shocked to see that he seemed to be considering this. "You guys, don't forget that in all the horror movies sex equals death."

Boris shrugged. "And yet somehow it worked for Beth and Kevin, didn't it?"

Angie didn't need to see or hear anything else to realize they were both serious. She wanted to protest that they couldn't afford people getting it on when they were supposed to be resting for their final escape out of town, but this was their down time, wasn't it? And they were both adults.

She wordlessly stood up as Boris and Jasmine scooted closer together and started making small talk. Thankfully, that was all they did until she was out of earshot. After that, well, that was entirely up to them.

Angie went up the shaky wooden stairs to the first floor. Kim was snoring softly on the floor nearby. Megan, on the other hand, shifted in the bed. Wordlessly, the young woman moved aside, making room for Angie if she wanted to join. After some hesitation, she did. Neither of them did anything with each other besides huddle together under the blankets for warmth, but that was apparently enough for both of them. Angie lost consciousness, feeling oddly content given the situation.

FOURTEEN

Angie awoke about an hour later to the sound of Beth screaming her name from down the stairs of the tower.

"Angie, get up here! You need to see this!"

She only mumbled for a second about having to leave the coziness of Megan's arms before she remembered what was happening and jumped out of bed. Megan sat up next to her, confused, while Kim was already up and staring through the door to the upper stairs. From below, she heard voices as Jasmine and Boris hissed to each other to get their clothes on so they could go up and see what was happening. Rudy stood at the bottom of the tower stairs, right by the front door, his hand tightly gripping Jasmine's gun.

"What is it?" Angie asked Rudy.

"I could only see a little bit through the front door," Rudy said. "You better go up top and see for yourself."

She ran up the clattering metal stairs, the entire thing shuddering under her weight as she went up them with far more speed than they were designed for. Her mind latched onto this, forcing her eyes to find the places in the walls and ceiling where the stairs were bolted it. This was nothing that would have passed a modern building inspection, and it was only allowed for the tourists with strict rules that they could only go up a few at a time, along with regular checks and maintenance on the stairs. It gave Angie an idea, a last minute Hail Mary they might be able to use if they found they had no other options left. She would get everyone preparing for it shortly if they had the time, depending entirely on what she was about to see.

At the top of the stairs was a short metal ladder leading to a wooden hatch above. She climbed it and had to shove hard at the hatch to open it. A small amount snow had accumulated on it and nearly frozen it shut, but it gave under pressure and allowed her up. This led her onto the narrow balcony that surrounded the light room itself, and she held onto the short railing as she made her way over the slick surface to the waist-high door. She had to get on her hands and knees to get through, but at least it was already open. Beth had been waiting for her.

The light room was a cramped, dreary-looking place, far removed from the romantic notion most of the tourists had of the beauty of lighthouses. There were mirrors along one half of the room, although they were there purely for show now as the high quality, super-polished ones were now shattered on the floor of the Mukwunaguk Historical Society Museum. The light in the center was also purely for show and could be turned on if there were power in the lighthouse, but the light it provided was weak and feeble compared to the lighthouse's glories of yesteryear. As though to give one last indication of how far the grand lighthouse had fallen, long thick strips of flypaper hung from the ceiling, leftover from a summer that had given birth to a particularly tenacious generation of insects. Old Bert should have taken them down ago but apparently he had never gotten around to it and now never would. The strips were brittle in the cold and held hundreds, maybe thousands of flies and mosquitoes, but they were still sticky enough that Angie had to duck to keep them from getting stuck in her hair.

"What is it?" Angie asked Beth. Beth, also crouched low to avoid the flypaper, was standing against one of the windows. The windows needed cleaning and the edges had a healthy growth of frost, but the snow had subsided substantially and it was still possible to see out to the main portion of the town across the small harbor. Beth pointed out the window.

"What do you see?" Beth asked.

"Uh, nothing."

"Exactly."

Angie understood what she meant. There should have been plenty of light coming across the harbor. Even if most people would have their lights off at this early hour (and according to Megan's phone, it had been shortly after three-thirty when she woke up), there still should have been street lights. Instead, the entire town was dark aside from the red-smoldering ruins of the café and the museum.

"How long has it been like this?" Angie asked.

"About ten minutes. I wasn't sure whether to call you. It might just be the storm blew down a power line, but then I saw something else and figured you needed to come up here. I think this might be what we were waiting for."

"Where's this something else?"

"Wait for it. Last I saw, it was in the direction of the chopstick factory."

Angie waited for thirty seconds before it appeared again, although it had moved significantly closer than the factory. There was a flare of light as something bright passed between the warehouses at the end of the harbor. It was vaguely human-shaped and seemed to be on fire, but it was too far away yet for Angie to make out many details.

That's the owner of my mysterious footprints, Angie thought. *That's Pestilence.*

As startling as it should have been to see one of the Four Horsemen of the Apocalypse walking around in the flesh (or whatever the hell it had), that wasn't even the truly frightening sight. The glow cast by the figure temporarily illuminated everything nearby, giving Angie a view of the horde that surrounded it. And the zombie horde had grown large indeed. It would only be a couple hundred strong at the most, Angie knew, just as she knew that probably meant every single other resident of Mukwunaguk was among them now. Those of them here in the lighthouse were all that was left.

And judging from the direction they were moving, every single one of them was coming this way.

Then the glowing figure disappeared behind another building. Without its light, Angie could no longer see the rest of the horde, but there was no doubting it was still there.

"Christ Almighty," Angie whispered.

"We're not going to get out of this, are we?" Beth asked quietly.

Angie's first impulse was to blatantly lie and say that of course they were all going to survive. Her second desire was far more fatalistic, the wish to tell Beth that there was no hope and they might as well give up. After a couple of deep breaths, Angie instead decided to split the middle. "I don't know. That doesn't look good. But I've got an idea that might help us survive for just a little bit longer."

"Does this idea involve me coming back inside? Because I'm freezing my tits off out here."

It did involve her coming back inside, at least for now. She sent Kevin back up as a lookout to take Beth's place. Someone needed to stay where they could keep an eye on the horde's movements. Angie was no longer worried that their lookouts might be seen. Judging from Pestilence's movements, she guessed that the Horseman (or was it Horsewoman?) knew exactly where they were. Given her predictions earlier, Pestilence had probably known their location this whole time. She had just been waiting for some reason, maybe because she wanted to make sure the rest of the town was cleared out of the living before she arrived. The lighthouse could very well be her last stop in Mukwunaguk before she declared her plague of zombies complete here and ready to move on to the rest of the world, a world where people foolishly believed there was such a thing as a "traditional" Romero-style zombie that they could easily dispatch with a shot to the head. That was a good way to guarantee the world burned.

Or maybe, Angie thought, Pestilence had waited this long because she thought it would better please her Legion, whoever they might be, if Angie's little band was slightly rested and better able to put up a fight. Maybe she had wanted the Legion to see the survivors interacting with each other so that it was more interesting when Angie and her friends died. Angie tried not to dwell on that for too long, though. They had no time left for that kind of thinking.

She let Beth stay inside and warm up while she, Rudy, and Boris went out to the storage shed and found all the tools they could, hammers and wrenches and screwdrivers, as well as some rope, chain, and bungie cords occasionally used for extra security on the fence or for hauling around heavy equipment. The rope and chain by themselves weren't long enough for what Angie had in mind, and the bungie cords would be too unreliable to use except in the most dire circumstances, but combined with some of the blankets and sheets they had gathered inside, they might be just enough.

Angie set several of the survivors to work on the ropes and chains while she gave others the tools and carefully instructed them in exactly what she wanted. This would be dangerous, she said, and if they did their job either too well or not well enough, it would probably mean their deaths.

While they set about their tasks, Angie gingerly went back up the tower and popped her head out of the hatch long enough to see how close the horde was. They had come around the end of the harbor and its warehouses, and the front part of the group could now easily be seen even though the snow had picked up again. The flickering red and orange light in the center of them all was clearly Pestilence, taking her leisurely time bringing the horde around. Nonetheless, Angie estimated they would be here in perhaps five minutes.

"Alright, come on down, Kevin," she said into the light room. "We need you briefed on what's going to happen."

"But who's going to watch for the zombies?" he asked.

"I don't really think we need to do that anymore, do you?"

Kevin came down with her and they all gathered in the dining room. Their makeshift beds had been dismantled and repurposed for Angie's plan, so the heap of rope and chains and sheets were in the corner waiting to be moved to their final location.

"Really?" Kevin asked after she went over it all one more time in front of everyone together. "That's your plan?"

"It's our final option," she said. "We only do it if we can't keep defending the lighthouse."

"That's not an option," Kevin said. "That's a good way to get us all killed."

"And if it comes to that, then our options are getting killed that way or getting ripped apart by zombies," Jasmine said. "I don't know about you, but Angie's way of killing ourselves seems quicker."

"I thought we didn't need to worry about the zombies anymore," Rudy said. "Isn't that what the pills were for?"

"Okay, I'm going over this for the last time," Angie said. "For one, we still have no way of knowing for sure that the pills are going to work."

"They won't," Kim said.

"Thank you, Kim. That's so incredibly helpful," Boris said.

"And B," Angie continued, "even if they do work, the only thing they'll do is keep you from becoming another zombie. And if they work the way I think they do, then they aren't even going to be very good at the job."

"What do you mean?" Rudy asked. "They worked well enough for you."

"Yeah, and I've been on them for years. They're in my system. Megan took one just before she was bitten, though, and we saw how that worked with her." Angie did her best not to let her rage rise at the nasty look Kim gave Megan. "So if they are what makes us immune, then you guys will probably have a reaction somewhere in between, although since you only each had one and that was a couple hours ago, it would likely mean that your reactions would be closer to Megan's. Anyone that gets bitten will probably need to get dragged around with us, and given what we're going to try, I can't imagine that working out well."

"So this is it, huh?" Kevin asked.

"Everyone just focus and maybe we can get through this," Angie said. "If we have to go with the fallback plan, I still think there's a possibility we can escape. Yeah, I admit it's a long shot, but for God's sake, we've actually made it this far. We can make it a little further."

Everyone stood around the dining room, waiting to see if she had more to say. Angie had to admit that, as far as troop-rallying speeches, it was hardly one for the ages, but it was the best she could manage at the moment. She was still tired, after all.

"Okay, so everyone get to their places and make sure you have your weapons." She put Rudy and Boris at the back door, while Kevin, Beth, and Jasmine manned the front. As she still probably wasn't in good enough shape for a fight, Angie had Megan take the mass of ropes and chains up the stairs and store them in the light room. Angie had the urge to stop her before she went up and kiss her, but the tender moment they'd had in bed hadn't quite been enough to justify such a thing yet. Maybe it was something they could explore if they both lived through this.

She had to think for a moment what she was going to do with Kim. Angie didn't think she would be of much use at either of the doors, but she wasn't sure if she wanted to take Kim out of the action completely. After a few seconds, she instructed Kim to grab the tools and be ready at the bottom of the metal stairwell. Kim was the thinnest and lightest of all of them, which meant she was the one best suited to set Angie's emergency plan in action should it come to that.

She heard Megan yell something down from the hatch. Angie couldn't hear exactly what she said but she didn't think she had to. Even with the wind still howling outside, she could still hear the crunch of feet in the snow outside. How many people did there need to be at once for her to hear them over the storm? There was some additional mumbling, the occasional chant of "Braaaaains!" or else non-verbal groaning. But the one sound she could hear clearly, through the wind and walls and doors and horde, what the raspy sound of a woman laughing.

"This is it," Boris said as he, Rudy, and Angie all turned to face the back door. "If this so-called Legion is watching us, this is our last chance to do or say anything to get them in our favor."

Angie shook her head, hefting Old Bert's gun in one hand and a garden hoe in the other. "I don't think that would do any good. I think this is exactly what the Legion has been waiting to see all along."

FIFTEEN

After some moments of thought, Angie put the gun in the pocket of her coat. They'd already seen how effective bullets really were against these things. The gun was nothing more than a last resort, really, a last suicide run that would likely end with everyone and everything inside the lighthouse going up in a literal blaze of glory.

And if they had to rely on her fallback plan, that was exactly what she hoped for. For now, though, the gun would be fairly useless. Nonetheless, she'd made sure that Jasmine still had hers just in case someone else needed to initiate the final plan instead of Angie. There was no guaranteeing she would get out of this, and she made sure both Boris and Rudy saw where she put the gun in case they needed to grab it if she fell.

Everything inside the lighthouse became silent. The only sounds were outside as the horde crowded closer. Then, peculiarly, even those noises stopped and there was just the storm. Had the entire horde of Mukwunaguk come all this way just to mill around outside the lighthouse like it was some kind of altar? Was it possible they didn't even know the last survivors were in here?

Before that hope began to take root in Angie, it was ripped away. It was difficult to be certain, but she thought she could hear a single set of footsteps approach in the snow at the back door.

"Angela and Boris," a voiced hissed. There was no mistaking it as belonging to anyone other than the one who had left the message on Megan's phone. "I know the two of you are there listening to me."

All three of them exchanged glances. Rudy looked confused, but Angie understood instantly and put a finger to her mouth in a shushing gesture. Although Rudy still didn't seem to understand, Boris nodded with a knowing look in his eye. This was just a further example of the butterfly effect that had been set into motion earlier in the evening. Megan, Beth, and Kevin weren't supposed to be here. And if they weren't, then Angie would have arranged the defenders at the doors differently. One of them would have been at the front door with Jasmine, although she wasn't completely sure why Pestilence assumed it would have been Rudy and not one of the others.

Pestilence, however, answered that question for her after a few seconds. "I trust that both of you have sufficiently recovered after your romp not too long ago. I hope it was enjoyable, too, considering for one of you it will be the last time you ever have sex."

Both Boris and Angie looked at each other with wide eyes. Boris looked like he was about to say something but she shushed him again. If they got out of this, she could explain, not that she was sure she wanted to. Apparently, according to Pestilence's plan, they'd been intended to sleep together from the beginning. Angie couldn't imagine any alternate reality where that might happen, but she thought she could see the twisted logic behind it. Pestilence seemed to be trying to entertain this Legion, and modern fiction was full of women reforming the bad boy. They always got together. That was the way the narrative worked. The guy wasn't supposed to instead make-do with the heroine's aunt, nor was the heroine supposed to spend her last night alive in the bed of another girl.

There were several seconds where Pestilence said nothing. Angie realized she was waiting for their response. In her perfectly planned scenario, this was supposed to be their chance to talk to her, to discuss what was going on. Her villainous monologue. After all, Megan wasn't supposed to have been there to tell them everything she knew.

"Um, hello? I know you're in there," Pestilence said.

Amused despite the situation, Angie motioned for the other two to stay silent.

"You are in there, right? Don't you want to know who I am and why I'm doing this?"

Angie was tempted to call out that they already knew, but it occurred to her that they would be better off the longer it took Pestilence to realize not all the tiny details she had seen were working the way they should. Not that she wouldn't realize that now, but the less they said, the more confusion they might place in their enemy. And Angie would take any advantage she could get now.

Pestilence sighed. "Screw it. Everyone, just go on and do your thing."

A pause, and then the zombie horde roared an incoherent approval. A few seconds later, the door rattled as an uncountable number of zombie fists slammed into it.

All three of them took a defensive stance a few feet from the door. The door was fairly sturdy, being rather new compared to the rest of the lighthouse to further discourage vandals or teenagers looking for places to drink and screw. The first shudder, however, told Angie that the door wouldn't hold out for long. Stoned teenagers were far different than the undead remnants of the entire town.

She could hear shouts from the other end of the building coming down the wooden stairs from the first floor. It sounded like maybe Beth was asking if they wanted the rest of them to come down. The only thing Angie screamed was to stay put. If they had to ask then the zombies weren't coming from that direction yet, but that didn't mean they wouldn't.

"Final chance for us to do a heroic last minute kiss," Boris said to Angie. He said it with a smile. Angie couldn't help but smile back.

"Get bent."

The door burst open.

Angie didn't even hesitate long enough to pick a target. As soon as the door was out of the way, she brought the end of the hoe down, its rusty metal blade coming down on the first zombie to try shoving through the door. It turned out to be Veronica, and the garden tool went straight into her chest just between the words "keep" and "calm." The hoe caught in her rib cage and Angie had to struggle to get it free. Veronica didn't appear to feel any pain but looked horribly confused that she had suddenly grown a new protuberance between her breasts. Angie didn't have time to find this funny, though, as a crush of zombies tried to push through the door behind her.

This, Angie had hoped, was what would keep them all alive for at least a little longer. Zombies weren't exactly supposed to be masters of battle strategy. In theory, their power was in their numbers. The narrow door, however, would prevent more than one or two from coming at them at a time. Unless the zombies suddenly developed the ability to plan, which, let's face it, was entirely a possibility given the rather vague rules Pestilence had applied to them, then this strategy would be sustainable for the short-term. Eventually it would collapse, though, and through sheer force of numbers the zombie would be able to power their way through. Angie had never thought she would be able to prevent that. They would certainly try, but that was where her back up emergency plan came in. It actually wouldn't work unless the zombies breached their early defenses.

Angie stepped aside, yanking the hoe out of Veronica as she did so. Rudy had an enormous pair of hedge clippers, and while Veronica was trying to regain her balance from the first blow, Rudy put the blades around her neck and snapped them shut. It would have been nice if her head had popped off and rolled away as easily as it would have in fiction, but instead the rusty metal only went partway through her flesh, probably getting caught on the bone. That was enough for now, though, as the damage was sufficient to send Veronica stumbling back into the push of zombies behind her. Betty was nearby, and there seemed to be just enough humanity left in her that Veronica's partial dispatching pissed her off. She tried to push through the other zombies but got stuck in the doorway with both Veronica and one other. Gina, Angie realized, the teenager who worked at the gas station in the evenings and had a tendency to wear t-shirts for rock bands that had already been ancient by the time she was born. Angie had always kind of liked her. She'd been the thoughtful type, always carefully considering her answers no matter how inane the questions.

Boris ran an ice pick into the girl's throat.

Angie was glad to see they were both heeding her advice to not mess up too much of the zombies above the neck. They still weren't completely sure how much damage the head had to take before a zombie burst into flame, but this early on, they couldn't risk it. That risk would come later.

It was hard to be certain over the din of the horde groaning and requesting her brains, but Angie thought she heard a commotion erupting from elsewhere in the lighthouse. The zombies had finally commenced an attack on the front door. That point would probably be even more defensible still, considering the zombies had to go up some railing-less concrete stairs to reach it. Hopefully, the defenders there would be able to hold out for longer than they would here, as the loss of that particular part of the lighthouse now would be devastating to their later plan.

Angie, Boris, and Rudy hacked at the zombies, trying to damage them as much as possible without attacking their heads, and as the precious seconds ticked away, Angie felt her strength diminishing quickly. She was fairly healthy but she had never made much point of working out, and she felt it now. Her lungs also burned with the sudden exertion. That would be her years of smoking catching up with her. She briefly thought about giving the habit up if she made it out of here alive, then realized a vow to herself made under these circumstances probably wasn't worth much.

Multiple zombies fell, their body's taking enough damage that they couldn't stay upright against the force of their brethren behind them, and when they went down it was into the kitchen, falling flat on their faces. The area just inside the door got crowded quickly as writhing zombie bodies began to stack up. They were still a hazard though, reaching out and trying to make cheap grabs at their three attackers. Angie and Boris occasionally redirected their attention the zombies piling at their feet in an effort to cut off a few of the hands reaching for them, but every second they spent doing that was time they weren't using against the ones still trying to get in, and they found the zombies slowly pushing their way through, some stepping on their fallen comrades and others pushing the bodies aside with the combined force of the horde behind them. Angie started to step back, glancing at her companions only long enough to be sure they were following her lead. She hadn't had a chance to consider exactly how long they should stay here holding the back door, but they wanted to retreat before there was no chance of getting up the stairs.

Angie's last-ditch plan required the zombies to get in, although it would work better if as many as possible were incapacitated. It looked to her now that they were about as good as they could get. "Time to go!" she yelled. The other two started to follow her as she retreated to the dining room, all of them still swinging their makeshift weapons in an effort to do as much damage to the zombies on their way out as possible.

Rudy swung a little too close.

It happened so fast that Angie didn't have time to put all the pieces together in her mind until a few minutes later. That was when she realized Rudy, with his hedge clippers wide open, got a little too zealous in going after one of the zombies that had staked a place just inside the door next the growing mound of incapacitated living dead. The zombie in question had been Lucas "Sugar" Shack. Angie hadn't known much about him other than his ridiculous nickname and the fact that Rudy was often complaining about him owing Rudy a significant amount of money for some long ago offense. One blade of the clippers took Sugar in the stomach, but they stuck there and in the few seconds where Rudy tried to yank them out two more zombies clawed at him, one getting a firm hold on his shirt while the other, unlikely as it might have seemed, grabbed him by the ear. The one with the ear pulled his head towards her before Rudy could react and, with the other hindering his movements, the zombie's mouth came down on the top of Rudy's head. Angie was fully aware that human teeth should have in no way been able to rip open a skull, but that was exactly what they did, making a very audible crunching noise before Rudy was pulled into the main mass of the horde at the door.

Then he was gone. The whole moment had lasted no more than a second. Angie didn't even have time to scream out his name.

She also didn't have time to mourn her cook. The noises up the stairs were getting louder, and the three defenders set to guard the front door were sounding increasingly worried. Now was the moment for a full retreat, and they needed to act panicked like it wasn't part of her plan at all. The panic, at least, wasn't hard to fake.

"Run!" Angie said. She wasn't sure if Boris could hear her over the moans of the horde, but he understood her body movements well enough when she turned and dropped the hoe to run.

Abandoning her weapon felt wrong, but she couldn't run effectively with the unwieldy thing at her side. Besides, she still had the gun, even if its time in the plan hadn't arrived yet.

She didn't bother to look back as she crossed the dining room and got the wooden stairs at the far end. She did look back as she started to go up though, and saw that Boris was straggling behind, a strange look in his eye that she didn't like. She'd seen that look in his eye before, had in fact seen it in a lot of men. It was the smug satisfaction they got when they suddenly believed they were the smartest person in the room and they had suddenly been blessed with an idea so brilliant that everyone else would bemoan that they hadn't thought of something so obviously wonderful first.

In Angie's experience, it was a look men typically had right before they made jackasses of themselves.

"Boris, whatever you're thinking of, don't do it!" she said over her shoulder as she ran up the stairs, stopping at the top to look down through the floor back at him. She wanted to tell him to stick to the plan, but it suddenly occurred to her that Pestilence, despite being heard at the back door right before the zombies had broken it open, couldn't be seen anywhere in the horde so far. There was no telling where she was or if she might be listening in, and Angie wanted to make it look like they were running around without any idea what they were doing for as long as possible.

Angie blinked in confusion as Boris slowly sauntered up to the bottom of the stairs and then proceeded to, well, do nothing but stand there.

"Boris, what the hell are you doing?" she hissed.

"I've got a theory, and it's kind of based on what you were saying earlier," he said. Although there was some stress in his voice, it didn't seem like nearly enough given the massive number of undead following right behind him. He turned around to face the horde, not doing anything at all. To Angie's shock, zombies surrounded Boris at the bottom of the stairs and just stopped.

"What the hell?" Angie asked.

"It's what you were talking about. All of this? It's just to entertain this so-called Legion." A single zombie came forward from the others, moving slowly as though he thought Boris was a dog that would bite any second. Angie tensed, waiting for something to happen, but Boris didn't move except to talk. He looked maddeningly confident in himself. "So the only thing we need to do is nothing."

"Wait, what?"

The single zombie slowly poked Boris with his finger. Boris still didn't move. "We do nothing. As long as we don't do anything interesting, we're not entertaining to those sick bastards. You know, the only winning move is not to play."

Angie watched as the zombie shambled back to the others and they moaned gently amongst each other as if conferring. She had to admit there was a certain crazy sense to what Boris said, but as soon as she thought about it for a few seconds she saw a glaring, horrible flaw in his logic.

"But Boris, isn't irony interesting?"

His head shot up to look at her, obviously startled that there might be something he hadn't thought of. "Huh?"

"If you just stopped right there thinking you'd found a way to be immune and you were wrong, then wouldn't the irony of you getting ripped to shreds be interesting?"

"Oh," Boris said. He took a slow step to the stairs, looking back at the zombies as they all raised their heads, their intimate conference over, and looked at him. "Maybe I should just…"

The zombies spilled over him at once. He was ripped apart with such force that his blood went all the way up the stairs and sprayed the front of Angie's coat.

She didn't stop for any length of time to mourn him. Maybe he hadn't been such a terrible guy after all. Of course, he hadn't been an especially good one either.

Angie threw some decorative lamps from the top of the stairs back down them. She knew they wouldn't stop the zombies for more than a few seconds, but seconds could honestly be all the difference between life and death at this point. As she ran through the living room, she heard Beth, Kevin, and Jasmine screaming to know what was going on. Angie was about to yell back that she was coming and they needed to get ready when she stopped short, staring at the foghorn.

Zombies can hear, right? she thought. She tried to think back to the rest of the night, searching for any memory that would suggest hearing was just as important a sense to the undead as any other. She couldn't remember anything specific, but what the hell. It was worth a shot.

"Cover your ears!" she yelled as she ran to the foghorn and grabbed the crank. It was unfortunate she didn't have any earplugs of her own, although she had to admit her death would be just as interestingly ironic as Boris's if she tried this and all it did was deafen her long enough for a zombie to sneak up on her.

"What was that?" Jasmine yelled back. The slamming on the front door told her that the zombies hadn't broken through yet. There probably weren't as many in front as there had been in back.

"I said, cover your..." Angie didn't finish. The first zombies had made it up from downstairs and were now surging into the living room with her, not so fast that she couldn't outrun them if she had the space and energy but quick enough that they could overwhelm her in just a few seconds.

Angie turned the crank. The old foghorn bellowed, a deep, vibrating thrum that shook the whole lighthouses, rattling the windows and instantly giving her a headache from its proximity. She only turned the crank four or five times, enough to ensure everyone in the vicinity with working eardrums would be stopped in their tracks. As she stopped turning, her hearing had gone fuzzy, but it had worked. Zombies might not feel pain when someone shot them, but they felt the piercing noise rattle in their brains. Several still had enough human reflexes to cover their ears, but most others staggered, a large number of them falling to the floor and twitching. Angie wondered only too late if that would be enough head trauma to set them aflame. Thankfully, though a few looked like there might be smoke coming out of their ears, none of them started on fire.

Angie ran from the foghorn to the front entryway, jumping over a couple fallen zombies just as they showed signs of getting back up. She could still hear commotion from downstairs as more zombies streamed in, probably ignoring their shocked brethren as they trampled them underfoot. That move had bought her some time, as well as allowing for more zombies to fit in the lighthouse. She just hoped none of them would crush the other zombies' heads before she and the rest of the survivors were in place.

Angie skidded to a stop in the front hall. The three defenders were still in front of the door while Kim, looking hurried and determined for the first time all night, worked off the bolts that connected the bottom of the metal stairs to floor. They'd loosened most of the bolts earlier to make her job easier now, but Angie saw even at her quickest speed this might not be enough.

"You've got to hurry!" Megan yelled from above. Angie looked up to see her head framed by the hatch, snow blowing in from above her. Only now, when Angie realized her life and the lives of everyone else down here would require them to run up all those stairs – yet *carefully* – did she get a sense of vertigo from the height. It was about three or four stories up, and an equally long way to fall down.

Angie looked at the defenders, making a quick judgment of each by speed and weight. "Jasmine and Kevin, get the hell upstairs. Beth, stay here and help me and Kim with the bolts."

Kevin looked like he was about to protest leaving his wife behind, but Beth gave him a quick peck on the cheek, a squeeze of his groin, and a short whisper in his ear. Judging by the way he blushed, it was a promise of something truly kinky should they both make it out of this alive. With no more hesitation, he ran up the stairs, holding Jasmine's hand as he did so neither of them would fall back down the steep spiral steps. The staircase rattled beneath them. It probably would have done that under normal circumstances anyway, since it wasn't designed to be used with that kind of speed, but it shook even more so now. That's what would happen when every single bolt trying to keep the thing steady had been loosened.

Beth grabbed another wrench like the one Kim had while Angie had to make do with a claw hammer. She looked back down the hall to the living room and saw that most of the zombies had gotten back up and where jockeying for room to come through the narrow hall and take the three people there that they thought were easy prey. Then she glanced at the front door. Despite the fine craftsmanship of the door, decidedly more so than the back door, the door jamb looked like it was cracking. Angie had been a little worried at that. The plan required the zombies to be able to easily get in through there, but if the door held up too well, that meant someone would have to open it for them. As it was, that didn't look like it would be a problem.

All the bolts that held the stairs directly to the floor had either been completely undone or else were loose enough that it didn't matter. Not every bolt needed to be completely undone. In fact, they couldn't be. The plan had been risky from the beginning, and had she had more time to come up with something, she didn't think she would have gone with something so desperate. The bolts needed to hold just long enough for everyone to get to the top of the tower. They then needed to give out immediately after. It was the kind of precision that didn't lend itself well to the situation. In fact, Angie realized that she'd missed something important: she'd thought to loosen the bolts on the first floor and all the ones that bolted the staircase to the wall, but they had completely neglected to do anything to the bolts that connected the stairs to the second floor landing. The landing was only a thin strip of wood with four places where the metal was bolted in, but it would be enough to keep the stairs stable when they weren't supposed to be.

"Kim!" Angie screamed. "The second floor!"

Kim looked up and, for a horrible moment, Angie thought she didn't understand and Angie would have to take precious moments they didn't have to explain. But Kim surprised her, running up the stairs to the second floor and kneeling on the landing, studiously working at the bolts with her wrench.

The front door broke open. The zombies who had come from downstairs had made it to the end of the hall. There was no more time to make sure the staircase was loose enough. Time for their final retreat.

A zombie came through the broken door taking a swipe at Beth with his fingernails before turning on Angie. Lenny, a local mechanic that Angie had slept with twice. He'd been a great date and gentle in bed but had a horrible tendency to drone on about hockey stats. Angie brought the claw of her hammer down onto his gaping lower jaw, smashing his teeth and forcing his mouth permanently open wide like a snake that had unhinged its jaw to eat. He staggered back, giving Angie the moment to turn and go up the stairs. Beth was ahead of her a few steps, and the combined weight of their harried footsteps made the stairwell shake and groan beneath them.

Angie was almost at head height with the second floor landing when one of the zombies reached up and gripped her ankle. Its grip wasn't strong enough to hold onto her for more than a second, but it still tripped Angie up. She slammed into the steep metal steps hard, almost slipping back down into the zombies that had started to try their way up the perilous stairs. Pain blasted through her, although she barely noticed in her panicked adrenaline rush. The force of her hitting the stairs caused the entire thing to shake far more than it had before. Out of the corner of her eye, she saw one of the nearby braces come away from the wall. The stairs were no longer supported by anything below the second floor, and most of the bolts above the second floor wouldn't hold its weight by themselves anymore. That meant Kim's work on the second floor landing was probably all that was keeping the giant metal contraption upright.

Angie had the sudden realization that this wasn't going to work. She hadn't had the time to plan out the loosening of the bolts. The stairwell needed to collapse, or at the very least break away enough that no one would be able to get up to the tower anymore. But someone had to stay behind and finish those last bolts on the second floor. Best case scenario, that person would get left on the second floor. Under any other circumstances, that might be considered safe, but not according to Angie's plan. They hadn't had time come up with an escape plan from the second floor. Anyone stuck there might be able to get out, but it was more likely that they would die.

"Kim, go up," Angie said. She was surprised how calmly she said it. She'd expected Kim to follow her orders without question. The expression Kim gave her, though, let Angie know that she understood perfectly what Angie was suggesting.

"No, you have to be the one up there. You have the gun."

"I can use it from here if I need to," Angie said. "And if I can't, Jasmine still has one."

"I'm lighter than you. I still might be able to get up."

Angie looked down at the zombies. The steep incline combined with the curved shape of the stairs had been hindering the zombies before, but just as they had been all night, the zombies stubbornly refused to conform to one set of rules. Pestilence must have known that it would provide a more intense situation if her pet zombies just for right now had enough coordination to climb the stairs. The first couple had rounded the spiral staircase about halfway up to the second floor. A few more had difficulties with the incline, tripping and falling back into the mass below. The zombies were now shoulder to shoulder in the lighthouse, jostling for room as they reached up at the two women still in their view. That was actually perfect, exactly what Angie had hoped. But it wouldn't do either of them any good if they were stuck here.

"Okay, fine, but hurry!" Angie raced up the remaining steps, gritting her teeth and muttering a prayer under her breath every time the giant tube of metal that was the spiral staircase shifted underneath her. She could see up here that most of the braces had come away from the wall. At the top the stairs, the metal buckled under her weight, dropping her several inches and causing her to screech. The metal held long enough for her to grab the ladder, though, and that at least was still bolted firmly to the wall.

Angie's initial impulse was to climb straight up and take a breather out on the frozen deck outside the light room. However, she didn't feel like she had the right yet. She had to stay here and watch, to make sure that this was going to work. She wrapped her legs and ankles around the rungs of the ladder, an uncomfortable position but nonetheless one that would keep her from falling. Keeping one hand on the ladder for balance, she let the other swing free so she could turn slightly in her position and look down.

From up here, the bottom of the tower looked like Hell, a pit of dead but moving and moaning bodies reaching up for her, waiting for her to fall. About twenty feet below her on the second floor landing, Kim was just standing up. All the bolts holding the staircase to the landing were gone, dropped to clink on the heads of the undead below. Kim hesitated, obviously not sure what to do. Angie was about to scream at her to stay on the second floor, that there were windows there she could jump out of with only a couple broken bones to show for it if that was her only means of escape. But before Angie could say anything, Kim saw the two zombies still making their way up the stairs. Panicking, Kim dropped her wrench and went back onto the stairs, moving as quick as she could to get up.

"Angie, what are you..." Angie looked up to see Megan's face through the hatch again. "Mom?"

Kim's unrestrained movement on the staircase was the last straw for it. Over the moans below, Angie could hear the distinct creak of metal shifting more than it should. The braces, though not attached to anything anymore, did well in keeping the metal cylinder in place in the center of the tower for a moment, then several of those braces bent. The entire staircase tilted to one side, dangerously catching Kim at the wrong moment and almost throwing her over the low railing. One of the zombies below her wasn't as lucky, tumbling head over heels off the side and hitting the zombies below with a meaty liquid *thwack*. The other zombie held on, although it didn't seem to know how to move on a visibly askew staircase.

Angie looked directly below and saw that the small metal platform that was supposed to be immediately below the ladder was now several feet away and also inching lower. The metal at the bottom of the staircase, already older than Angie herself by many, many years, was giving up under the abuse and buckling. Just like Angie had planned, except she hadn't thought one of their own would still be on it when it did.

"Kim, hurry!" Angie screamed. "You can still make it." Even as she said it, though, she realized she didn't actually believe it. If she had, she wouldn't still be here on the ladder. She would have gone up and out of Kim's way, giving her a clear path.

Angie was, however, in a position to grab Kim if it came to that. Her muscles tightened, bracing her closer to the ladder as she held out a free hand to Kim. Kim saw it and, despite the weird angle of the stairs, went up them faster than Angie would have thought possible. That extra effort probably hurt her rather than helped her, though. The staircase groaned again, and just as Kim reached the top, something vital underneath gave way.

Kim jumped, reaching out for Angie's hand as the stairwell broke down and collapsed completely, raining twisted metal on the zombies below. Kim caught Angie's arm in the middle of her forearm. Angie grabbed back, but Kim's arm was too thin and slick with sweat, giving Angie little to hold on to. Kim grabbed at Angie's coat with her other hand, pulling Angie down at an awkward angle. Kim may have been light, but Angie still didn't have the strength to hold her for long with just one hand.

"Mom!" Megan screamed and reached down through the hatch, but she could only barely touch Angie, let alone Kim as she dangled over the pit.

Angie looked down into Kim's face and her piercing blue eyes. For a moment, she looked crazed and terrified. Then it passed, and she looked more calm and clear than Angie had probably ever seen her.

"Look away, baby," Kim said up to Megan.

"Mom, no, we can still—"

"Megan Jean Howzer, you look away this instant, and that's an order!"

Angie glanced up just long enough to see Megan, her face stricken, pull away from view. When she looked back down, Kim had let go of Angie's coat.

"Kim, don't. I can still pull you up." Even as she said it, she knew it wasn't true. Despite Kim's scrawny frame, Angie didn't have the strength to pull her up with just one arm, let alone help her up the narrow ladder.

"I've seen the way you look at Megan," Kim said. Angie almost would have expected some derision in her voice, but there wasn't any. The woman just sounded resigned. "Promise me you'll look after her. Even if nothing happens between you, keep an eye on her."

There wasn't anything other for Angie to say than, "I will."

"Oh, and stop taking that Big Pharma crap. That stuff will kill you."

With that, she let go and fell into the mass of squirming zombies and twisted metal.

SIXTEEN

Angie extricated herself from the ladder and climbed up, careful of the slightest bad movement that might slip her up and send her tumbling down to join the sounds of tearing and chewing below. Once she was through the hatch, she collapsed into the snow on the deck, breathing deeply as the adrenaline rush of everything that had just happened caught up with her. She couldn't let the tiredness take her over yet, though. They still had the second half of the plan to execute, and it was probably going to be even more dangerous than the first half.

Still, she understood that every one of them needed to take this moment to appreciate that they had survived up to this point. And also, no matter how brief, a moment to mourn their dead.

Angie got up to her knees to see Megan, also on her knees, staring blankly at the open hatch behind Kim. Angie thought for a second that she couldn't imagine what she was going through, but she supposed that wasn't true. Angie remembered full well that moment she had seen her father die. Megan's moment, however, was probably full of a lot more complex emotions.

"Megan?" Angie asked.

Megan didn't answer. Angie became aware that she could still hear the zombies below as they ate and tore apart something wet. Angie turned to close the hatch, although she knew she would have to open it again shortly as they began the final part of their plan.

"Megan?" Angie asked again.

"I'm fine," Megan said. The flat tone of her voice indicated to Angie that she was most likely not fine at all. She was probably in shock and denial. Angie stood up, touched Megan lightly on her shoulder as she carefully walked around her to the other side of the deck, and crouched down to get into the light room.

She did not find things going as well as she had hoped. Jasmine, Beth, and Kevin should have all been readying their rope and chain contraption. Instead, Beth was sitting on the floor, her back against the wall as she shivered furiously. It was indeed cold up here, but her pale pallor suggested more than just an adverse reaction to the weather.

"What's going on?" Angie asked.

"Look," Jasmine said, holding up one of Beth's limp hands for Angie to see. She had to squint to see it in the dim light, but it was definitely there: a darker line against the pale skin of the back of her hand. A scratch. So simple. Yet from a zombie, theoretically deadly. Upon closer inspection, Angie could see that it smoked a bit, but the skin around it wasn't taking on the same charred color as most of the full-on bites she had seen.

"I think this proves that you were right," Jasmine said. "Those pills you gave us seem to be what kept you and Megan from turning into zombies."

"But it hasn't been in her system long enough or in big enough doses," Angie said. This was a problem. A big one. The final part of their plan didn't have any room for someone who could barely stand, let alone climb.

"She's going to live, though, right?" Kevin asked. For the first time all night, Angie thought she heard genuine, heart-felt worry in his voice. He gently stroked Beth's other hand, occasionally stopping just long enough to smooth her hair and give her a gentle peck on the cheek. Beth only seemed to be partially aware that any of them were there. Most of the time she just stared blankly ahead, whimpering every so often at some hallucination or trick of the dim light that only she could see.

Under any other circumstances, Angie would have answered him in the affirmative with no hesitation. But this was different. It looked like she would survive the zombie infection in much the same way Megan had, but that was no longer the number one threat against them. In the next few minutes, their biggest worries would be getting burned alive or falling to their deaths, and Megan wasn't in the position to protect herself from either.

Instead of answering him, Angie just said, "Jasmine, get the ropes ready. I'm going to go check that everything else is in place." She didn't give any further instructions to Kevin. There was a very good possibility that they were all about to leave his wife behind to die, and if that was the case, Angie wanted him to have these last few moments.

Angie crawled back out onto the deck, being careful not to slip on the snowy mush and fall over the short railing. That would come soon enough, but hopefully in a lot more controlled manner. As she made her way around the round deck back to the hatch, she looked over the side, for the first time actively judging the distance from here to the ground. She wasn't good on making estimates about height, but she thought it was about forty to fifty feet. From certain areas of the deck, there would be a shorter drop if someone fell, only about ten or so feet to the sloped roof of the house itself behind them, but that wouldn't do any of them any good considering the state she intended the entire lighthouse to be in shortly. There had been enough snow over the last couple hours for it to start drifting against the walls, but it wasn't deep enough that it would help break any falls. A drop from all the way up would be deadly, or in the best case scenario would break enough bones that whoever fell wouldn't be walking away. That was the first obstacle. The second was the zombies themselves. As Angie followed the railing around the circular deck, she looked at the zombie concentration. From the tower, it was hard to see the area directly behind the house, but given the height, she could otherwise see everything all the way across the flat ground from the harbor on one side and the security fence on the other. Given that she'd known an entire town's worth of zombies would be here, she hadn't expected the area to be completely clear, but there were still more zombies roaming around outside than she would have liked. It would be impossible for a couple hundred zombies to all fit in the lighthouse, but with them crowding both the bottom and first floors, she'd hoped they would all be concentrated enough for the final part of her plan. There were enough still wandering around outside in random groups that she was no longer sure, though.

There was also no sign of Pestilence. Angie saw some footprints in the snow that might have been deeper than the others, but it was impossible to be certain with how much the zombies had been tromping it down.

Back at the hatch, Angie found Megan still kneeling. She had scooted closer to the hatch, as though she wanted to look through it for any last trace of her mother, yet knew that she really didn't want to see. Angie put a hand on her shoulder again and gently whispered that Megan should go inside and help Jasmine. Megan wordlessly stood and went in. Angie only got the quickest view of twin lines running down her cheeks that might have been tears slowly on their way to freezing.

Angie looked back down through the hatch, hoping she wouldn't see any of Kim's grizzly remains. She saw some fresh blood on the walls in a few spattered places, but that was thankfully all that didn't appear to belong to the zombies themselves. There was one piece of luck, at least, and that was the fact that much of the twisted metal from the staircase had come to a rest right near the front door, effectively blocking most of the zombies from getting out there. There were even a few still trying to crawl over the wreckage to get inside. That was good enough. Angie didn't want to wait for much longer. If they did, the zombies could start realizing there was nothing more for them to eat in here and they might as well wander out and on to the next town. Not that Angie would be particularly upset about the loss of Ontonagon, but there were other towns beyond it that she didn't have a long-held irrational dislike for. And once this whole thing spread, it would be near impossible to stop it. If this particular zombie apocalypse was going to be stopped, it had to happen right now, right here, on probably the last occasion where all zombies were in one place.

She went back around to the door and crouched to peer inside. "Jasmine, how's the rope?"

Jasmine had tied their rope-like contraption around the light in the center of the room. In her moving around, she'd gotten one of the nasty strips of flypaper stuck in her hair, and rather than trying to pull it out she'd just left it there, dangling like a carnivorous ponytail that had a curious appetite for insects.

"It's about as sturdy as it's going to get," Jasmine said. Judging from her expression, that wasn't very sturdy at all. They'd cobbled it together from the ropes and chains and bed sheets, and the resulting item could be called a rope in only the loosest sense of the term. The stronger the material, the closer they'd put it to the top of the rope, with the chains wrapped around the light then going to the ropes and finally the sheets at the end. The idea was that if some part of it gave out under their weight, they wanted it to give out closer to the bottom of the tower where there was less chance the fall would kill them. They'd even found a use for the bungie cords, using all of them to further strengthen the point where the chain was tied to itself. All they needed to do now was throw the rope over the side and climb down. From there they could run.

As if it were all that simple. Angie didn't think she'd ever climbed up or down a rope in her life. It never looked hard in the movies, but she knew better than to trust that. And they also had to take care of the zombies. Simple enough, in theory. The instrument of their own destruction was built into them. It was just a matter of using it without Angie and the others killing themselves in the process.

And then there was Beth.

"I'm not going," Kevin said as Angie came in.

"What?" She almost asked why, except that was obvious. Beth was breathing heavily and from the way she blinked at her husband, Angie guessed she was a little more present than she had been just before. The fact that they had all taken the pills hours earlier rather that immediately before she was scratched must have helped her, but Angie still estimated it would take her more time to fully recover than they had. They needed to go now before the zombies had a chance to break up and scatter.

"I know you're going to leave her behind," Kevin said. "I know why. I understand. But I'm not going without her. If she has to stay then so do I."

The heroic sacrifice for true love. Given how much Pestilence had engineered this entire thing as an entertaining story for the Legion, Angie should have expected something like this. Yet her gut reflexively clenched against the notion. She'd already watched three people die right in front of her in the last few minutes. That should have been more than enough for an entire lifetime, yet it wasn't even all the death she had witnessed in just this one night. And they had all been more or less under her protection. How a waitress had become these people's protector she didn't know, and she felt like she had been doing a rather poor job of it. Becca, Old

Bert, Johnny, Rudy, Boris, and Kim. All dead because of her.

And yet, she realized, that wasn't the whole story. Here were three people in front of her that weren't even supposed to be there. According to Pestilence's plan, the only people that were supposed to be in this tower probably should have been Angie and either Jasmine or Boris. Beth, Kevin, and Megan were all supposed to be dead or part of the zombie horde by now. Hell, even if she was supposed to be here Beth was still supposed to be turning into a zombie right now, and Angie's thinking had prevented that. It had to count for something. Somewhere along the line, she had to have done something right. And she could keep doing it.

"No," Angie said to Kevin. "You're not staying."

"Angie, you can't force me to leave her. If this—"

"She's coming with us."

Everyone looked up at her, Kevin and Jasmine with surprise, Beth with confusion, and Megan with, despite the obvious grief still playing over her face, a look of admiration.

"How the hell do you propose that?" Jasmine asked.

"I honestly have no fricking idea. But I know I'm not losing anyone else tonight. I swear it." She turned around and shouted out the short door into the blustery night. "You hear me, Legion? Not one more! Not one more of these people is going to die for your amusement."

The wind howled back, as though it were interested to see if she could back up such a boast.

"Okay, but how?" Jasmine asked. "Beth's not in any condition to hold the rope. Hell, I don't know if any of the rest of us are."

Angie thought about this for a second. Kevin might be the only one with the strength to carry her, but only under the most ideal circumstances. Going down a rope cobbled together from bed sheets in the middle of a snowstorm was not ideal.

"She goes first," Angie finally said. "We tie the rope around her and lower her. The rest of us then climb down it one at a time."

"She'll be a sitting duck if a zombie comes for her while the rest of us are still up here," Kevin said.

"That still gives her more of a survival chance than being left up here."

"How does that affect the rest of the plan, though?" Jasmine asked.

"Honestly, I have no fucking idea," Angie said. "I'm playing this entire thing by ear."

They all did their best to tie the bed sheets around Beth under her arms. She was just conscious enough of what was going on that she didn't fight them, although she seemed completely confused and scared at the bizarre flurry of activity around her. Once she was secure (or at least as secure as possible when her entire survival relied on the tensile strength of sheets), Angie dragged her out onto the deck. Everyone else ducked through the door and joined her. It occurred to Angie that, in this lighthouse that was nearly a hundred and fifty years old, this was the last time anyone would ever be in that room.

The deck was only designed to hold one person at a time, so all five of them made for a terribly crowded and terrifying experience. All it would take was for one of them to slip in the snow, maybe reflexively reaching out for one of the others and sending them both to broken necks. Angie did one last check to see the placement of zombies on the ground. There were none here on this side of the house by the tower. Perfect.

"Alright, everyone get ready to lower her over the side as soon as you hear the gunshot," Angie said. "If it looks like any of our knots are about to give out on her, lower her faster instead of trying to bring her back up. She'll have more of a chance to survive that way. As soon as she's on the ground, the next person needs to climb down. Only one at a time, because I don't think this thing can hold that much weight at once. Jasmine, you go down after Beth so you can use your gun to defend her if needed. Then Kevin, then Megan so there might be people to help if your strength goes out and you fall. I'll go last. Everyone understand?"

There were nods all around, although their silent ascents were partially obscured as the wind blew a particularly harsh gust of snow across their faces. Angie had really hoped the storm would have calmed by this point, but she should have known better. Pestilence and the Legion would think it was much more interesting for the finale to take place in the storm.

"Okay, get ready," Angie said. "I'm off to take care of our friends." She went around the deck to the hatch and opened it, staring down with a faint sense of vertigo at the zombies still milling about at the bottom. They looked like they were getting restless. The promised feast was not here. They would never be getting it, either. Angie pulled the gun from her pocket, struggled to get a good grip on it with her stiff, cold fingers, and aimed it down through the hatch. All it would take was a single bullet in one of the many heads, but she aimed specifically for one that was near the mangled wreckage at the door. It wouldn't be able to get out that way, and it would block anyone else trying to do the same.

Angie took a deep breath.

"Angie! No! Wait!"

The words were lost in the wind for a few seconds, just long enough that Angie didn't register them until after she had squeezed the trigger. The gun fired and one of the zombie's head exploded from above. Erupting from the wound, right along with brains and blood and bone fragments, was a furious fire.

Angie turned to see Megan coming around from the other side of the deck. "What?" Angie asked. "What is it?"

"The way's not clear!"

"What?" Angie asked. She looked back down through the hatch. That single zombie had immediately gone up in flames, catching two next to it and quickly spreading to the wall. Every zombie in the building, hopefully every zombie from the entire town, was going to go up like tinder over the next minute. The lighthouse was going to go with them. They no longer had any time to wait, let alone time to clear out a rogue group of zombies suddenly blocking their path.

Angie went around the deck to see that a small group of zombies had wandered closer to the front from the back of the lighthouse. They were still moving, heading for the area where Beth would touch down when they lowered her. It was hard for Kim to see if they were looking up at the survivors on the tower, but even through the snow, Angie could see the lead zombie's bright Hawaiian shirt. Archie, the last of the four original zombies.

"No, no, no. We can't have this," Angie muttered. It might have been her imagination but she thought she could already smell the burning from beneath them. Between the massive number of highly flammable zombies inside and the lighthouse's old building materials, this whole place would go up quickly. Now their only escape route was going to be blocked.

Angie closed her eyes and gripped the railing tight, trying to think.

"Hey, do you see something else moving out there?" Jasmine asked.

There had to be a way out of this. This was Pestilence's show, and if she were really trying to make this entertaining for some soulless group watching them all, then she had to follow certain rules, right? There must be something that they could do or something that could happen.

"I think so," Kevin said. "Can't make it out, though. Looks kind of small."

Angie thought back to everything she had ever read, especially things about storytelling techniques. There had to be something built into the narrative that they could use. What was that storytelling device called? A Chekov's Gun, she remembered. Something that would have been introduced earlier, seemingly innocuous, that would become supremely important now.

"There's no way that's what I think it is," Jasmine said.

"It does seem kind of unlikely that he would find his way all the way out here."

Or maybe this would be the time in the story for that other age-old storytelling technique, the Deus Ex Machina. Something that comes out of nowhere, exactly the right thing happening at exactly the right time. Angie dismissed that idea, though. She didn't think Pestilence would be that lazy.

"Angie, are you even paying attention?" Kevin asked.

"Not now, guys, I'm trying to think."

"Angie, for the love of God, just look!" Jasmine said.

Angie opened her eyes and looked where Jasmine was pointing. There, bounding toward the lighthouse and effortlessly wiggling through a hole the zombies had left in the fence, was Doug. His tale wagged so enthusiastically that it left a squiggly-snakelike pattern in the snow after him. He stopped just long enough to look up at the tower, right at Angie, and bark a happy greeting.

"No, I won't sleep with you," Angie said with a happy smile. As if to say that he was okay with that, Doug barked again.

Right on cue, the five or six zombies below them turned to the noise and began moaning. Doug bounded away on his tiny legs, taking a long circuitous route in the general direction of the back of the lighthouse. The zombies shuffled along after him.

"Now, while they're distracted!" Angie said. They wasted no time in lifting Beth and, with the greatest precaution not to snag and undo any of the knots on the railing, they played out the rope to lower her down. Under other circumstances, Angie would have preferred to do it slowly, but the smell of smoke was absolutely not a figment of her imagination now. A quick glance up showed her oily black smoke streaming up from the other side of the deck as it vented through the hatch. It might have been the exertion, but Angie also felt an increasing heat to combat against the freezing wind. There was a noise growing from below them as well, actual moans of pain from the zombies that strangely complimented the dreary song of the wind.

Beth came to a rest in the snow at the base of the tower. Nearby, through the front door, there was a strong flickering glow that was only getting brighter with each passing second. There was no time to make sure Beth was safe or in a good position. It would be less than a few minutes before the entire lighthouse burned down with them still on top.

Jasmine went next, obviously scared shitless of intentionally going over the other side of the railing but not having the time to consider how much danger she was truly in. Although Angie would have preferred that they go one at a time to ease the strain on the rope, she saw now that they didn't have the time. Once Jasmine had half-shimmied, half slid precariously down the rope, Angie ordered Kevin to follow her. After he'd gone down a few feet, she heard a larger commotion somewhere near the back. The zombie moans and growls reached a crescendo and there was the unmistakable sound of ripping flesh, loud enough that Angie could hear it even over a particularly loud gust of wind. This was followed by distinct canine whine that went silent.

Oh Doug, Angie thought, and had a peculiar urge to cry that had been greater than almost any other time over the course of the night. As Jasmine reached the bottom and began untying Beth, though, Angie heard the sounds of the zombies growing louder briefly before growing softer again.

Angie looked out toward the fence and saw Doug running away. The ripping hadn't been him getting torn apart by the zombies. It appeared to be the other way around, in fact. Doug had a twitching dismembered zombie arm clutched between his teeth. The zombies shambled after him as though trying to get it back, led by the now one-armed Archie.

"Good boy!" Angie shouted at him. Doug paused just long enough to look in her direction, wag his tail furiously, and then turned around and sped off faster than his little legs should have been able to carry him. The zombies trailed after. The survivors might have troubles with those remnants later, but for now the way was clear to escape.

Angie gestured for Megan to go. "Now, before anything else realizes we're sitting ducks over here."

Megan looked dubiously at the rope. "I'm not sure I can do this."

"Can you smell that?" Angie asked. "Can you *feel* that?"

Megan paused, then nodded. There was no mistaking it for a trick of her mind anymore. The temperature on the deck had gone up several degrees, and there was a rancid burned stench halfway between a campfire and scorched flesh.

"We have no choice. And I know you can do it. Because I know what you were going through on that shore yesterday. I know because I've been there. And anyone who hasn't been there wouldn't know what we know."

"And what's that?" Megan asked softly.

"That deciding to live can be the hardest thing people like us ever do. And you made your decision. So are you going to let the decision be reversed right now without even trying?"

Megan looked at her for a couple more seconds. Instead of saying anything, she gripped the rope and lifted her leg over the railing.

"Good," Angie said, having to raise her voice both not just over the wind now but the growing roar from the building beneath them. Glancing over at the rest of the lighthouse, she saw the light of flames glowing bright from most of the windows, even the ones they had covered. The fire had already burned away their meager handy work. "Now go! I'll be right behind you!"

For one horrible moment, Megan looked like she wasn't going to be strong enough to hold on to the increasingly slick rope. She slid a couple of feet and cried out at the rope burns on her palms, but she managed to stop her descent in favor of something slightly more controlled. There was a sound from the lighthouse something like an explosion, and several of the windows shattered to spit flames out into the night. The smoke here on the deck was thick enough now that Angie couldn't help but cough. She waited until Megan had gone down about fifteen feet before she herself took hold of the rope and climbed over the railing. There was no more time to wait. The lower levels of the lighthouse were all ablaze, kindled by the majority of the town's zombies. The tower wouldn't last much longer at this rate. If Angie didn't start making her way down now, she might never get the chance to.

Angie wrapped her legs around the rope – which was still actual rope this high up – and started shimmying down with slightly more control than Megan had shown. Right as her eyes were level with the deck, she heard something loud bang from the other side of the light room, just outside her view. If she hadn't known better, she would have thought something was coming up from the hatch. But there was nothing that could have climbed all the way up the inside of the blazing tower without the benefit of a fire extinguisher and an extremely long ladder.

Unless, of course, it was something that didn't necessarily need to conform to standard rules of logic. Angie didn't want to see what it might be. She scurried down the rope faster, stopping only long enough to look down at Megan's progress.

Looking down was a mistake. Angie had never been particularly afraid of heights, but given the circumstances – trying to escape a burning tower on a makeshift rope while a furious snowstorm off Lake Superior make the rope slick with ice and also tried to blow her off into the darkness – she thought she had the right to suddenly develop new phobias. Jasmine, Kevin, and Beth were all waiting at the bottom and staring up at them anxiously. Kevin appeared to be limping like he had slipped and fallen the last few feet, but it had hardly been life threatening. Jasmine had her gun ready in her hand but there was nothing around for her to point it at. Megan had just gone past the halfway point, probably at the point now where she would live if she fell. As Angie watched, though, one of the knotted bed sheets just above Megan's head started to slip.

"Megan!" Angie screamed, pointing at the loosening knot. Megan looked up and saw it, then immediately started sliding down the rope faster. The movement only seemed to loosen the knot more, but before it could give way completely, Megan let go. She dropped the remaining ten feet and landed with a roll that obviously dazed her but otherwise didn't seem to cause any significant damage. *Good*, Angie thought. *They're all safe. I did it. I kept them alive.*

"Angela Zwiersky, you didn't give me the proper chance to introduce myself earlier."

The voice was raspy, thick, the husky tones of someone who'd once had a beautiful voice but had ruined it with years of chain-smoking. It came from above, impossibly clear despite the noise of the storm and the fire. Even though she knew she didn't have the time, Angie only looked up slowly, not wanting to confirm what she thought she would see.

But there she was standing on the deck, her hands on the railing on either side of the rope. She was exactly as Megan had described her, and yet merely hearing the description hadn't been enough to make Angie picture this impossible person. It was impossible to determine her height, given Angie's weird angle of staring straight up at her. Flames had erupted from behind the woman, but she would have been easy to see in the darkness even without the blaze because she gave off her own soft glow, like the embers in a fireplace shortly before they went completely out. She was naked from head to toe but any possible naughty details had been burned away, the spot between her legs smooth and her breasts charred to the point where Angie couldn't see any nipples. The woman's skin was black and cracked, highlighted with red burning just below the surface.

But her most striking feature was her back. A pair of wings looked like they had sprouted from there at one point, but they had either been ripped or burned away, leaving boney, flapping nubs fluttering behind her.

"I am Pestilence," the woman said. "One of the Four. And I am here in service of—"

"The Legion," Angie called up. "Yeah, yeah, I know." She did her best to ignore the horror staring down at her and instead looked down again. Somehow that had now become the better view.

"Wait, how can you know that?" Pestilence asked. Angie looked up only long enough to see a look of pure shock appear on the demonic woman's face. She seemed to be looking past Angie for the first time to the survivors on the ground.

"No. No that can't be right," Pestilence said. "This isn't the plan. This isn't what the Legion wants to see."

It took all of Angie's mental strength not to say something snarky. She was about one third of the way down the tower. Still high enough that she wouldn't walk away from a fall.

"Angela Zwiersky, what have you done?" Pestilence screeched. "How did you make this happen? You and Boris are supposed to be all that's left! You're supposed to be the only one who survives the night!"

Angie still resisted looking up, but she didn't like that tone. Pestilence was already somebody she didn't exactly want to make angry. And from the sound of her voice, Pestilence was beyond merely angry and heading into the territory of righteous fury.

"This is not the formula! This is not the way a zombie story is supposed to work!" Then, in a worried voice that was almost childlike, "The Legion is going to be so mad at me."

Angie let herself slide down a little, ignoring the pain from the rope on her hands. Just a little farther.

The rope jerked underneath her and Angie had to grip it tighter to keep from toppling. She looked up to see Pestilence touching the rope where it went over the railing with the tip of her finger. The rope had begun to smolder.

"Oh God," Angie muttered. Screw safety. Screw pain. She had to get down the rope now.

"I don't know how you did this, Zwiersky, but you'll pay for it. I don't care about formulas and final girls anymore. I'm in charge of this scenario, and I'm sick and tired of you trying to defy it." The rope jerked again and Angie could hear it audibly straining under her weight. "You're going to die, and then every single one of your friends down there is going to die with you. All of you dying will be more pleasing to the Legion than too many of you living."

Angie got below the level of the knot that had been unraveling. The rope was now buckling under her weight in two different places. A quick look down showed she had about twenty feet to go. Come one, come on…

The rope gave out. She didn't know from which point, nor did it matter. All she knew was that for a couple moments she was in free fall, and then pain lanced through her entire body. The snow was just thick enough here to cushion her fall somewhat, but not enough that she didn't feel multiple bones throughout her body break. She screamed, a sound that didn't come out anywhere near as anguished as she actually felt. Her vision went dark and blurry for several seconds, the pain intense enough that she suffered a very brief blackout.

That state didn't last long as Pestilence's scream of fury woke Angie all the way back up. From her place sprawled on her back, she had a clear view all the way up the tower. The fire had broken through the walls in several points and the entire top deck looked like it was on fire. Even in the snow, Angie felt her hair scorch from the heat of the burning building, now bright enough to light up the entire night around them. There were multiple moans and screeches coming from inside as the remains of the townsfolk burned.

But all these sights and sounds were nothing compared to the vision dropping down from the top of the tower. Pestilence's faint glow had turned into a full blaze, making her look like she was burning from the inside out. She jumped over the railing, but rather than dropping straight down, she seemed to glide on the wind as though the broken vestigial remains of her wings were still capable of flight. At about twenty feet from the tower, she went into a dive, at faster than free fall. She hit the ground a short ways behind them, causing an impact that shook the earth and pelted them all with dirt and rapidly melting ice. It reminded Angie of what Megan had said happened at the shore. She thought of Pestilence's wings and her impact and thought *fallen angel*. Was that what Pestilence was? Was that what all the Horsemen of the Apocalypse were?

As much as Angie wished she had time to speculate, she knew her life depended right now on being able to get up and away from the burning woman stomping toward her through the snow. Every step vaporized the snow beneath her feet, surrounding her with plumes of super-heated steam. Angie tried to roll away, but even that simple motion caused her unbearable pain. The pain was everywhere in her body, which Angie supposed was technically a good thing. If she could feel pain everywhere, it meant her back was not among the broken bones. All the other breaks, however, would keep her from getting away.

"Was it really so hard?" Pestilence hissed. "Is it ever that hard? I have a plan. I know how I'm going to entertain the Legion. But you people always fight it. Always."

Pestilence stopped right next to her, standing over her and sneering. Angie again tried to move and again nearly blacked out from the pain.

"I'm not doing this to be horrible, you know," Pestilence said. "I'm doing this because the Legion needs their entertainment. They'll get it from me or they'll get it from someone else. And people need to suffer for them. It was never anything personal against you. It was just my duty."

Pestilence reached down and grabbed Angie by the throat. She lifted Angie up with a strength that shouldn't have been possible with her fire-shriveled body. "Except now it is personal. Now I actually want you dead." She held Angie up so that Angie's toes only barely touched the ground. The fingers around Angie's neck burned and she thought she could smell the cooking of her own flesh. "You don't have the slightest idea what and who you've really been messing with tonight."

"No, and we don't care!" Jasmine yelled from behind Pestilence. Before Pestilence could turn to look at her, Jasmine had leaped and wrapped something around Pestilence's eyes. Pestilence dropped Angie in confusion, sending another fresh wave of agony through her, but she landed so that she could clearly see what Jasmine had done. She'd taken the nasty strip of flypaper that had been stuck in her hair and wrapped it around Pestilence's eyes, pulling it tight so the sticky brittle paper adhered to the Horseman's eyeballs themselves. Pestilence howled and threw Jasmine off her back, but the flypaper stayed even as it smoked and caught fire on Pestilence's face. Jasmine plopped and rolled in the snow, but even though she didn't look hurt she didn't move, instead defiantly staring at Pestilence and yelling for the Horseman to come get her.

"No," Angie muttered, not even having the strength to raise her voice. "Jasmine, don't." She couldn't let this happen. She had become their leader. Their protector even in some ways. If Aunt Jasmine let Pestilence kill her, then Angie would have failed.

Megan stooped next to Angie, grasping her hand. "Don't move," she said quietly. "It's our turn to protect you."

As Pestilence turned and blindly took several steps toward Jasmine, the soft explosion of a gunshot pierce through the wind. Pestilence staggered back a couple feet in the direction of the burning lighthouse. Angie looked to her right to see Kevin, Jasmine's gun now in his hand and pointing at Pestilence's chest. Pestilence looked for just a moment like she was in pain. Apparently, she didn't have the same ability to shrug off bullets that her zombie creations did.

Megan pulled the gun out that Angie'd been keeping her in her pocket. After making sure the safety was off, she too took up a position with Pestilence between her and the lighthouse. She fired a few more shots and Pestilence's left breast exploded, spraying a viscous red and orange fluid that looked suspiciously like thinned-out lava. Pestilence staggered back again, nearly falling to her knees yet just barely managing to stay upright. That was actually to the Horseman's detriment rather than benefit, as she wouldn't have been able to go any farther back if she had been on the ground. Instead, she crouched and then sprang at them.

Kevin and Megan both unloaded their guns into Pestilence, sending her flying back and crashing through the straining wall of the lighthouse.

Pestilence vanished into the flames and writhing zombies. She must have hit something load-bearing inside, because the second floor caved in on top of her, then the roof. The entire middle section of the lighthouse collapsed.

They all stood and sat there silently in the snow for several minutes, waiting to see if she would come back out. By the time they were certain she was well and truly gone, the wind had died down and the snow had eased back to flurries.

SEVENTEEN

On their way back into town, they found the zombies that had escaped in their pursuit of Doug. Whatever force had been keeping them hot and animated must have disappeared right along with Pestilence, because they had collapsed and been mostly drifted over with snow. One of the zombies, thankfully covered up enough that Angie couldn't identify the person, looked like it had frozen and fallen over while trying to do the Moonwalk. The only one Angie could see clearly was Archie, a strangely goofy grin now permanently frozen on his face. His frozen body was still reaching out for something, as though he thought it was still possible to get his severed arm back.

"It's kind of sad," Megan said. "I mean, I know we didn't know him like we did everyone else who died, but he was still a person before Pestilence got him. Do you think he was a librarian like the others?"

"I thought I heard Old Bert say on the day they came to town that this guy was actually a lawyer."

"Oh," Megan said. "Maybe that's not quite as sad as I thought."

As a group, they had trudged as far as the first warehouses at the end of the harbor. Although they had all decided they still needed to leave town and get help from the outside world, it had been agreed that they no longer needed to get there on foot. Nor did it seem like they needed to do it immediately, now that they were certain the zombies were all gone. That was a good thing, too, because none of them were in any condition for a long hike. At best, several of them were cold and getting dangerously close to hypothermia. Beth was still groggy and stumbled around, but she managed to keep going with the help of her husband, who lovingly caressed her hair as she leaned on him.

Angie was in the worst condition. While some of what she had initially thought were broken bones turned out to be less serious, she still believed she had at least one cracked rib and any attempt to put weight on her left foot made her hiss in pain. Once they saw the zombies frozen in place, she agreed to let the others go on ahead. They could find a vehicle they could all use and then come back for her. Then the five of them would leave Mukwunaguk, possibly forever. They still had no idea what story they were going to tell the authorities, but even in the unlikely event that people believed the town had been the site of an abortive zombie invasion the town would still likely be on lockdown, one giant crime scene that they wouldn't want to return to even if they could.

While Angie insisted that they all go on ahead, Megan would hear nothing of it and stayed behind as the others went back into town. They found a relatively dry place under the overhang of one of the warehouses and sat down on the pavement. Angie had to lower herself gingerly, Megan by her side the entire time and squeezing Angie's hand anytime the pain became too great. Finally, after much uncomfortable shuffling, they were sitting next to each other against the wall. It took Angie several seconds to realize how close they were to each other. She supposed she could try telling herself they were just doing it for the warmth, yet she knew that wasn't true.

"I'm sorry, Megan. I'm so sorry," Angie croaked. Her throat was raw from all the smoke from the lighthouse. Ironically, it made her crave nicotine, but she had somehow lost the last of her smokes in the mad dash through the lighthouse.

"Sorry about what?" Megan asked. Her voice was soft and distant. Angie had no doubt that Megan knew exactly what she was talking about.

"If you don't want to talk about Kim—"

"No, I don't," Megan said sharply. Tears welled up at the corner of her eyes. "I'm not ready to talk about that, okay? It's just…my relationship with her was already a complicated Hell. It's, uh, probably going to be a long time before I can talk about it at all."

With that she broke down crying. Angie made no more effort to push the subject. She just hugged Megan tight to her side, ignoring the shooting pain in her ribs, and let her cry into her shoulder.

Megan cried herself out after a few minutes. For a little while longer, they both sat in silence. Finally, Megan said, "I have to tell you something."

"Yes? What?"

"Um, I've always had a crush on you. Ever since I started to realize I wasn't into men."

Angie nodded. She wasn't terribly surprised. What did surprise her was that Megan, oh so timid Megan, took that moment to lean forward and kiss Angie gently on the lips. Angie was so caught off guard that she barely had time to try returning the kiss before Megan pulled away.

"Just in case," Megan said.

"Just in case what?" Angie asked.

"Just in case you decide anything you said or did tonight didn't count. You know, because we were in danger. I just wanted to enjoy it one last time."

Angie's only response was to take Megan's chin in her hand, turn the young woman back to face her, and plant a much longer kiss on Megan's lips. It didn't become anything more. There was no deep passion behind it, at least not now. That might come later. For now, they were both exhausted and in various degrees of mourning. A make-out session would have to wait until later, at least until after Angie didn't feel like she had knives sticking throughout her entire body.

Something barked at them and they both pulled away from each other, startled at the sudden intrusion into their quiet moment. Angie looked in the direction of the noise and saw Doug happily trotting toward them. The arm they had previously seen him absconding with was gone, but Angie noticed that his front paws were covered with dirt and snow. He had probably buried the arm somewhere like a prized bone. Someone, at some point in the near or distant future, was going to go digging in the wrong place and find an unpleasant surprise.

"Doug!" Angie called to him. "Good boy! Come here."

She'd expected the little dog to walk to his customary distance from her and then stay there, yet instead he walked right up to her and let her scritch him behind the ears. It occurred to Angie that, whoever Doug's actual owner might have been, that person had to be dead.

"Who's a good boy?" Angie said as he cuddled up between the two of them. He cocked his head at her as though he was desperately curious to find out. "You are! But I still won't sleep with you."

"Huh?" Megan asked.

"Never mind. Long story."

"So, uh, what happens next?"

Angie had no response. She didn't have the slightest clue what any of the survivors would do now. She didn't know where they would go or how much truth they would tell about tonight. She didn't know what would become of her and Megan, or even if she would keep Doug. She only knew one thing for certain, and that knowledge was too terrible to share with Megan in this tender moment.

She knew that Pestilence had only been one of four.

EPILOGUE

The sun is up, just peeking over the horizon. It's been several hours since the final confrontation at the lighthouse, and it will be several more before the first federal investigators show up trying to make sense of all this. They won't succeed in much, although in the following days the media will make much of all this, insisting it was a terrorist attack. Why terrorists would bother with a town the size of Mukwunaguk will never be explained. A few sharp armchair warriors out there will start to put it all together, although they will usually mix it in with their favorite conspiracy theories and steer the narrative far away from the truth.

For now, though, the remains of the lighthouse are quiet. The storm has stopped completely, but every so often the wind off the lake picks up enough to rattle some of the loose charred timber sticking up from the ruins at odd angles. This is what appears to be causing the shifting of burned wood and blackened zombie bones for several seconds, but it goes on for far too long to be anything other than something beneath it all trying to get out. After many minutes of this, a hand finally claws its way out of the soot, shifting the debris until the hand's owner is finally able to pull herself above it all, and Pestilence rises.

Then Pestilence promptly falls, tumbling out of the piled ruins and sprawling ignominiously in the snow. Her body temperature is no longer enough to melt the snow around her. Her glow has dimmed to practically nothing, and any terrible beauty she might have once had is gone. Instead, all that remains is something that looks suspiciously like the blackened zombie corpses around her. She moves weakly, trying to crawl away from the lighthouse remains. It's not obvious where she thinks she's going. Maybe she's fully aware she's not going anywhere.

Finally, when she's on an open patch of ground, she stops and takes a deep breath. Her lungs wheeze and her breath makes a whistling sound through the bullet holes in her chest. Her zombie creations might have been immune to such things, but she is not.

Then she speaks. "I know you're there."

Nothing responds to her but the wind and sounds of waves on Lake Superior crashing against the shore.

"Yes, you. You who've been watching and listening to this whole thing. I know you're listening to me now. I know what you are."

You stare across the worlds and realities at her, curious what she's doing.

"You and the rest of the Legion. All of you can hear me. Did I give you what you wanted? Didn't all that death and mayhem entertain you?"

Pestilence's arms start to crumble as she reaches out for you, but obviously the distance between is too far for that, not even measurable in any terms currently known to the human world.

"Please, you can't let this happen to me. This can't be how it ends."

Her hands crumble to dust. Her arms are following, and so are her feet.

"Were the zombies too fast? Too slow? Not traditional enough? I can do better next time. Just let me come back in my next form. I swear, if you let me do this again it'll be amazing. Please..."

She loses too much integrity to speak in anything more than garbled screams, but even as she collapses into nothing, her eyes continue to stare across the vast spaces of the world right at you. Pleading. Asking for another chance to entertain you and the rest of the Legion.

Then she's gone. The wind blows away her ashes and all that remains is a single, hard, round object. The closest thing the twisted being had to a heart.

There is just enough heat in it to melt the snow underneath. Once it touches the ground, the dirt appears to liquefy beneath it, allowing the Horseman's core to vanish into and join with the Earth, possibly to never be seen again.

Or maybe it will be.

THE END

CHECK OUT OTHER GREAT ZOMBIE NOVELS

Z BURBIA
by **Jake Bible**

Whispering Pines is a classic, quiet, private American subdivision on the edge of Asheville, NC, set in the pristine Blue Ridge Mountains. Which is good since the zombie apocalypse has come to Western North Carolina and really put suburban living to the test!

Surrounded by a sea of the undead, the residents of Whispering Pines have adapted their bucolic life of block parties to scavenging parties, common area groundskeeping to immediate area warfare, neighborhood beautification to neighborhood fortification.

But, even in the best of times, suburban living has its ups and downs what with nosy neighbors, a strict Home Owners' Association, and a property management company that believes the words "strict interpretation" are holy words when applied to the HOA covenants. Now with the zombie apocalypse upon them even those innocuous, daily irritations quickly become dramatic struggles for personal identity, family security, and straight up survival.

ZOMBIE RULES
by **David Achord**

Zach Gunderson's life sucked and then the zombie apocalypse began.

Rick, an aging Vietnam veteran, alcoholic, and prepper, convinces Zach that the apocalypse is on the horizon. The two of them take refuge at a remote farm. As the zombie plague rages, they face a terrifying fight for survival.

They soon learn however that the walking dead are not the only monsters.

CHECK OUT OTHER GREAT ZOMBIE NOVELS

900 MILES
by S. Johnathan Davis

John is a killer, but that wasn't his day job before the Apocalypse.

In a harrowing 900 mile race against time to get to his wife just as the dead begin to rise, John, a business man trapped in New York, soon learns that the zombies are the least of his worries, as he sees first-hand the horror of what man is capable of with no rules, no consequences and death at every turn.

Teaming up with an ex-army pilot named Kyle, they escape New York only to stumble across a man who says that he has the key to a rumored underground stronghold called Avalon..... Will they find safety? Will they make it to Johns wife before it's too late?

Get ready to follow John and Kyle in this fast paced thriller that mixes zombie horror with gladiator style arena action!

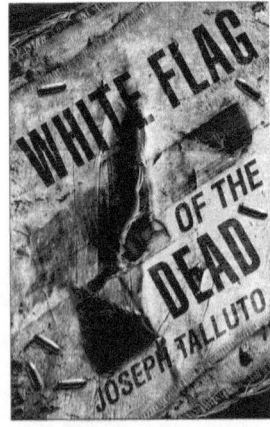

WHITE FLAG OF THE DEAD
by Joseph Talluto

Millions died when the Enillo Virus swept the earth. Millions more were lost when the victims of the plague refused to stay dead, instead rising to slaughter and feed on those left alive. For survivors like John Talon and his son Jake, they are faced with a choice: Do they submit to the dead, raising the white flag of surrender? Or do they find the will to fight, to try and hang on to the last shreds or humanity?

CHECK OUT OTHER GREAT ZOMBIE NOVELS

DEAD ASCENT
by Jason McPhearson

The dead have risen and they are hungry...

Grizzled war veteran turned game warden, Brayden James and a small group of survivors, fight their way through the rugged wilderness of southern Appalachia to an isolated cabin in the hope of finding sanctuary. Every terrifying step they make they are stalked by a growing mass of staggering corpses, and a raging forest fire, set by the government in hopes of containing the virus.

As all logical routes off the mountain are cut off from them, they seek the higher ground, but they soon realize there is little hope of escape when the dead walk and the world burns.

CHAOS THEORY
by Rich Restucci

The world has fallen to a relentless enemy beyond reason or mercy. With no remorse they rend the planet with tooth and nail.

One man stands against the scourge of death that consumes all.

Teamed with a genius survivalist and a teenage girl, he must flee the teeming dead, the evils of humans left unchecked, and those that would seek to use him. His best weapon to stave off the horrors of this new world? His wit.

CHECK OUT OTHER GREAT ZOMBIE NOVELS

RUN
by **Rich Restucci**

The dead have risen, and they are hungry.

Slow and plodding, they are Legion. The undead hunt the living. Stop and they will catch you. Hide and they will find you. If you have a heartbeat you do the only thing you can: You run.

Survivors escape to an island stronghold: A cop and his daughter, a computer nerd, a garbage man with a piece of rebar, and an escapee from a mental hospital with a life-saving secret. After reaching Alcatraz, the ever expanding group of survivors realize that the infected are not the only threat.

Caught between the viciousness of the undead, and the heartlessness of the living, what choice is there? Run.

THE DEAD WALK THE EARTH
by **Luke Duffy**

As the flames of war threaten to engulf the globe, a new threat emerges.

A 'deadly flu', the like of which no one has ever seen or imagined, relentlessly spreads, gripping the world by the throat and slowly squeezing the life from humanity.

Eight soldiers, accustomed to operating below the radar, carrying out the dirty work of a modern democracy, become trapped within the carnage of a new and terrifying world.

Deniable and completely expendable. That is how their government considers them, and as the dead begin to walk, Stan and his men must fight to survive.

CHECK OUT OTHER GREAT ZOMBIE NOVELS

DEAD PULSE RISING
by K. Michael Gibson

Slavering hordes of the walking dead rule the streets of Baltimore, their decaying forms shambling across the ruined city, voracious and unstoppable. The remaining survivors hide desperately, for all hope seems lost... until an armored fortress on wheels plows through the ghouls, crushing bones and decayed flesh. The vehicle stops and two men emerge from its doors, armed to the teeth and ready to cancel the apocalypse.

TOWER OF THE DEAD
by J.V. Roberts

Markus is a hardworking man that just wants a better life for his family. But when a virus sweeps through the halls of his high-rise apartment complex, those plans are put on hold. Trapped on the sixteenth floor with no hope of rescue, Markus must fight his way down to safety with his wife and young daughter in tow.

Floor by bloody floor they must battle through hordes of the hungry dead on a terrifying mission to survive the TOWER OF THE DEAD.